LOST VALLEY

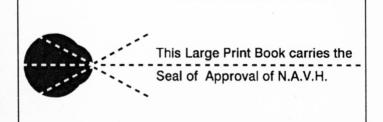

This Large Print Book carries the
Seal of Approval of N.A.V.H.

LOST VALLEY

LAURAN PAINE

WHEELER PUBLISHING
A part of Gale, Cengage Learning

Detroit • New York • San Francisco • New Haven, Conn • Waterville, Maine • London

GALE
CENGAGE Learning

Wheeler Publishing Large Print Western.
The text of this Large Print edition is unabridged.
Other aspects of the book may vary from the original edition.
Set in 16 pt. Plantin.

LIBRARY OF CONGRESS CATALOGING-IN-PUBLICATION DATA

Paine, Lauran.
  Lost valley / by Lauran Paine. — Large print ed.
    p. cm. — (Wheeler Publishing large print Western)
  ISBN 978-1-4104-4988-7 (softcover) — ISBN 1-4104-4988-2
(softcover) 1. Large type books. I. Title.
PS3566.A34L67 2012
813'.54—dc23   2012018163

Published in 2012 by arrangement with Golden West Literary Agency

Lost Valley

I

The Pawnees called it Larahipu, which was their word for traders, but while they meant it as a designation of the people who lived in Lost Valley, the mountain men who first saw Lost Valley thought the Pawnees had given that name to the valley, not the Arapahoes who lived there. Then the mountain men corrupted Larahipu into Arapaho, and down the years Larahipu Valley became Lost Valley. The Arapahoes disappeared, but James Hyland, who had first reached Lost Valley with Ashley's buckskin buccaneers when the entire territory belonged to Mexico, built a log post on Arapaho land, settled down, and prospered. James was a canny trader, but more than that he had arrived in the New World from stony Scotland where rich, good land was as scarce as new money, and James's feeling for land drove him to acquire as much of Lost Valley as he could.

James died in his bed at eighty-eight leaving to his only son Angus his settlement, which had grown out of the log trading post, and forty thousand acres of open range land. Angus created Lost Valley Ranch, added more thousands of acres to it, sold the post and most of the town of Hyland, built a great stone house on Lost Valley Ranch, brought in pure-bred bulls to upgrade his thousands of razor-backed Texas cattle, and went to his reward at sixty-eight leaving to his only son Douglas not only Lost Valley Ranch, more than a hundred thousand acres, but a legacy of complete solvency.

The ranch was still growing when Douglas stepped past his grandfather's moccasins and into his father's cowman's boots. Lost Valley Ranch was all Douglas knew. It was also all he cared to know. He was a powerfully built man of average height and smoky blue eyes. He had come to manhood astride horses, knew more about hard work in all kinds of weather than he knew about almost anything else, although Angus had forced him to spend four years in the East at school. In the town named for his grandfather, people knew Douglas Hyland as a rich, unsmiling, taciturn individual as honest as the day was long, strictly fair in all his dealings, and uncompromising in what he expected of life, and people. He employed nine range men. His foreman, Joe Lamont, did all the hiring, and Joe was the blindly loyal vassal of the lord of Lost Valley. He hired only top hands, men who would serve Hyland interests as though they were their own. Joe ran Lost Valley Ranch as though it were a kingdom, and in many respects it was, and always had been. Lost Valley Ranch had a two-acre cemetery a mile southwest of the main ranch yard where Hyland riders had gone into the ground after shoot-outs with Indians, renegades, rustlers, and anyone else whose temper was aroused at being ordered off Hyland land.

In town, people respected Douglas Hyland, avoided disputes with his nine range men, and viewed Joe Lamont as a shadow of his employer. It had been said often in town that no one had to like the men of Lost Valley Ranch, but the best way to get along, and to profit from getting along, was to give them plenty of respect. Fear certainly was part of that respect, but the main reason people respected Douglas Hyland and his men was because, according to Douglas Hyland's strict rules, his men did not become troublesome in town — or, if they did, they were fired the very next day — and the ranch had always been one of the largest contributors to the town's economy. It still was, but less so now than during the previous two generations.

The town had grown inevitably since it was located near good water and bisecting roads. There was timber one day's wagon ride northeastward in the mountains, and the next closest town to Hyland in Lost Valley was sixty miles due south, down where the Army had had a post and fort in the early days. Down there at Bridgeport a spur of the railroad tracks made a sashay past a solid two acres of corrals and loading chutes. Bridgeport was larger than Hyland, primarily because of the spur tracks. Cattle came from hundreds of miles to be shipped out of Bridgeport, and this could have obtained at Hyland instead of Bridgeport except that the earlier Hylands had absolutely refused to permit tracks across even the remote parts of Lost Valley Ranch. They had always guarded their privacy, their cow domain, with fierce resolution, and they still did. Douglas was a fair, occasionally susceptible man in many ways, but any mention of trespassing and he became something altogether different. As Joe Lamont had once summarized it for Sheriff Hatfield: "Treat Mister Hyland fair and there's no better friend on earth. Double-cross him or edge over onto Lost Valley land, and a man'll have trouble every Monday morning for the rest of his life."

Hatfield knew it was the truth because he'd rescued more than one incensed pot-hunter, wolfer, or squatter who had in mind fighting back.

Evan Hatfield had always said the same thing to them: "You go on over to the saloon, look for the toughest-looking, orneriest-faced, worn-down leather-hided son-of-a-bitch in there, and he'll be a Hyland rider. Then you multiply him by nine and that'll give you an idea of what you'll be up against if you get troublesome with Lost Valley Ranch."

Once, seven years earlier, a free-graze cowman out of New Mexico had trailed four hundred cows and long yearlings over Lost Valley Ranch on a northward course to Montana. That time, when Joe Lamont ordered them off before sundown, they had shot the horse from beneath Joe and gone into camp five miles farther along in the willow breaks of Arapaho Creek, and, before dawn, when they were rolling out and reaching for their boots, they had looked up into the closed-down faces of eleven men on horseback, sitting like stones, with their carbines pointed and cocked.

Douglas Hyland, wrapped in a blanket coat, had asked which of those men had fired on his range boss. When the leathery free-grazers had come up to their feet to fight, what followed, according to the free-grazer who had hired those cowboys, was a near massacre. By the time Sheriff Hatfield got out there to make a formal investigation, then rode back to town, Lost Valley Ranch was loafing around town in full force, and the free-grazers flatly refused to sign a complaint, and denied ever saying there had been a fight.

Evan and Douglas Hyland crossed to the saloon, got a bottle, took it to a table. When Evan Hatfield sat down to remonstrate, hard-eyed, square-jawed Douglas Hyland had said: "There wouldn't have been a fight if they hadn't wanted one. I don't make trouble and I don't allow my men do it. I run a cow outfit, Evan, and they work it for me. We mind our business. If someone comes onto my land like those men did, they get run off. That's all there is to it. I'm the law on Lost Valley Ranch and you're the law everywhere else."

Evan had had two drinks with Douglas Hyland without saying a word about the free-graze fracas. Without a signed formal complaint all he could have done in any case was grumble and growl, and with a man like Douglas Hyland that was pointless. They were friends, had been for quite a few years, but Hyland rarely socialized in town and Evan Hatfield only rode to the home place when he had business out there. It was an easy, comfortable arrangement. And, too, Sheriff Hatfield had over the years almost no trouble with Hyland riders, and that was worth something because most of the other cow outfits on the periphery of Lost Valley Ranch, that hired seasonal range men, could not control their riders when they arrived in town of a Saturday night with a pent-up week-long thirst and urge to hooraw the place.

The last time Evan Hatfield had been summoned to Lost Valley Ranch it had not been by Lamont or Hyland, but by some local people who saw a straggling, ragged band of Indians establishing one of their ragtag camps along Arapaho Creek, and had hastened to town to tell Evan so that he could get up there and chase them off before Hyland's men found them. Evan had ridden hard to reach the *ranchería* first and failed. Douglas and Joe with five of their riders were already over there, sitting their saddles, silently watching from a rolling land swell, and down along the creek Indians were noisily going about their unkempt camp, with eight or ten strong hearts also sitting their horses out a couple of hundred yards, between the Hyland men and the creek.

Everything was there, armed, defiant Indians, better-armed and rawhide-tough cattlemen. One spark would have started the fight when Sheriff Hatfield rode between the groups, snarled at the Indians to go back to their camp and put down those guns, then walked his horse toward the cowmen on the land swell. He did not look back but he knew without doing so that those strong hearts had not moved, had not obeyed him.

Douglas Hyland nodded at Evan without speaking. Joe Lamont and the other range men took their cue from Hyland; they, too, nodded without speaking. Back a mile or two, westerly, two riders were driving a recalcitrant old wicked-horn cow toward the creek. Evan watched this, then turned toward Hyland.

"The Indians go after that old cow?"

Hyland, gloved hands atop the saddle horn, shook his head. "No. I sent the men to find an old gummer and drive her down there." At the sheriff's stare, Hyland gestured. "Did you ever see anything like that? I remember them with good horses, healthy kids, good buckskin instead of those calico rags."

His horsemen drove the old cow to the camp. When the Arapahoes gathered uneasily to stand like statues and watch, one of the riders shot the old cow. The other one gestured with his hands, then they turned and loped toward the waiting men on the land swell. The Indians called back and forth; old squaws ran for their fleshing knives. They were already drawing the blood and rolling back the hide before Hyland's herders reached the land swell, and those strong hearts, looking back, then forward, finally came close to talk. All but one of them turned back. That lone Arapaho cradled his worn-out Winchester, drew himself very erect, rode toward the land swell, and, when he was about five hundred feet distant, he raised one arm high, palm forward.

Douglas Hyland did the same. Not a word was spoken. Then the strong heart turned back, and Sheriff Hatfield rummaged in a vest pocket for his makings and went to work rolling a smoke.

Douglas Hyland said: "We couldn't wipe them out, Evan. We tried for fifty years and couldn't do it. But we took everything they had." Then he turned, finally, toward the sheriff. "How'd you happen to be out here?"

Hatfield trickled smoke, looking down where Indians were swarming over what remained of the old gummer cow. "Some passers-by saw them trailing over your land and hurried down to tell me before you found 'em." Hatfield turned and smiled. "You're right, we took everything they had. . . . Well, I got to get back."

II

Evan Hatfield was a large, big-boned man who carried his better than two hundred pounds handily. He was powerful enough to break a jaw with either fist, and even-tempered. He had come out of Missouri thirteen years earlier, had buried his wife along with a lot of other emigrants down along the Missouri River bottoms, and had never remarried. He had gone from freighting to law enforcement by accident, and had been a lawman ever since.

Hatfield knew the law. Every snowbound winter for ten years he'd read law books. But in summary all that he'd read led toward a conviction he'd had before he'd ever seen a law book. People knew right from wrong. All a ton of law books did was try to define each instance, which lawyers loved to do, and which worthwhile people did not need a definition of because they inherently knew what they should not do. That was how Evan Hatfield administered the law in his territory, and in a way he was not very different from Douglas Hyland. He would not argue with lawbreakers; he would simply enforce the law against them.

But the Thursday morning it rained and the dawn stage came in an hour late because the creeks were all above their banks, Evan Hatfield met a gangling, straw-haired man with button shoes, a curly-brimmed derby hat, and a raw-boned, rangy build packed down inside a gray two-button coat. His name was Enos Orcutt, and, as they sat talking in Hatfield's office, one of the fundamental differences of right and wrong came more and more to Evan's attention. It was not a case of someone doing wrong when they knew what was right. Enos Orcutt unfolded a map, placed it in front of Hatfield atop the desk, and pointed to a small square almost in the center of the map, which had been traced out in blue pencil.

"One hundred and sixty acres, Sheriff, bordering on that unnamed creek, properly filed on at the Land Office over in Denver. What I want to know is how exactly to find it."

Evan silently rolled and lit a smoke. Then he said: "You got the homestead papers, Mister Orcutt?" When Orcutt brought forth the thick envelope and emptied it, Sheriff Hatfield said: "That's not an unnamed creek."

"It's shown that way on the plans at the Land Office in Denver."

"Then they'd ought to send some map-drawers down here," muttered Evan, reading the papers of homestead compliance. "That's Arapaho Creek." He smoked, read, killed the cigarette finally, solemnly folded the papers, re-inserted them into the envelope, and held it forth. "Mister Orcutt, before you go out there, I think you'd ought to stay in town and rest up for a spell."

The raw-boned, fair-complexioned man pocketed his map and envelope, eyed Sheriff Hatfield steadily for a moment. "Someone else is squatting on my land, is that it?"

"No. But someone else is using that land, and has been using it for over fifty years. Three generations of them."

The raw-boned tall man was not indignant. "It happens. They told me at the Land Office it happens very often."

Evan leaned back with a silent sigh. "Yeah, I suppose it does. You hang around town, Mister Orcutt, and I'll ride out there."

"I'll hire a horse and go with you. I want to see my. . . ."

"No. You stay here!"

Orcutt's steady gaze hardened slightly. "You don't believe they'll give up the land, Sheriff?"

"I want to explain things first, Mister Orcutt. . . . Loan me the map, will you?" The folded rough paper changed hands. As Sheriff Hatfield held it, he said: "What in the hell did you file on land down here for? It's cold in winter, blazing hot in summer, and a hundred and sixty acres isn't a drop in the bucket to what a man needs to make a living in Lost Valley."

"It'll be a start, Sheriff. I've been through Lost Valley before. I traveled for a gun company as a peddler for six years. I always liked Lost Valley."

Evan Hatfield nodded a little. "It's nice to travel through, for a fact, Mister Orcutt, but . . . a gun salesman? You aim to open a store here in town?"

"No, I aim to work my land and put up a house."

"Are you married?"

"No." The younger man smiled. "I don't need a family. I just want to settle down and get my hands dirty, Sheriff. I've always wanted my own piece of land, and with emigrants coming out of the East in droves now, I figured I'd better start building my place before all the good land was taken up."

Sheriff Hatfield knew emigrants. There were quite a few of them passing through nowadays, and some were even taking up foothill land on the outer boundaries of Lost Valley. But this was not the same at all. That one hundred and sixty acres was approximately where he had sat watching Douglas Hyland give those starving Indians an old gummer cow. It was not a matter of right or wrong. Orcutt's homestead application was in order, his map was correctly drawn down to the exact scale, along the township corners and proper metes and bounds. But that happened to be Lost Valley Ranch land, and from what Evan Hatfield knew of the Hylands, they did not surround free-graze in order to control it, the way most of the large cow outfits did, the

Hylands held deeds. That was how James, then Angus, and now Douglas operated. They bought title. It wasn't right versus wrong; it was clearly someone's mistake.

He told Enos Orcutt where the rooming house was, saw him pointed in that direction, then Evan went down to the livery barn. The rain had stopped, but the heavens were gray, and the ground under his horse's hoofs was soggy, in some places sticky and clinging. Also, there was a raw little north-to-south wind blowing about belly-high to a tall man.

He made fair time and fortunately his encounter with the stranger named Orcutt had occurred early in the morning, otherwise he would not have reached the great stone house before midafternoon, which meant he would not have been able to return to town until well after dark, and in raw weather that was not something a man accustomed to ordering his life so that he could avoid being out in raw weather did not cherish. Most of the riders were gone when he rode into the yard, past the buildings and up the slight incline to the big stone house with its elegant horse-head tie posts set at intervals beyond the broad sweep of verandah. One rider was leaving by the carved oaken front door when Sheriff Hatfield tied up. He and the rider nodded, then Douglas Hyland stepped forth to watch and wait, and, as Hatfield approached, Hyland said — "Coffee's hot in the study, Evan." — and led the way.

Why a single man required such a

magnificent house was an unanswered question through Lost Valley. Inside, no expense had been spared; the furniture was from the East, the oil paintings were massively framed and obviously of considerable value, even in the eyes of someone like Sheriff Hatfield who knew nothing about art. The study had a great stone fireplace and rich-toned leather chairs. It also had a large old carved desk. That was where Douglas Hyland filled two cups with black coffee and handed one to the sheriff as he gestured Hatfield to one of the big chairs. Then Hyland stood gazing at his guest, the formalities over with, as far as he was concerned. But he followed range custom. Instead of asking pointblank why Hatfield had ridden to the ranch on such a raw day, he said: "The rain was welcome, eh?"

Evan swallowed hot coffee before replying. "To range men it was. To me, well, I'd prefer it to rain only at night, and to dry out before morning." He smiled.

Hyland nodded without returning the smile and went to the edge of the massive desk to lean. "Trouble?"

Evan sighed. He would have preferred to just sit in the warmth of the room and sip his coffee. Now, he set the cup aside, dug out Orcutt's map, strode to the desk, and spread it out. Hyland looked, leaned for a closer look, and pointed with a blunt finger at the blue-penciled square. "What is that?"

"It's a hundred and sixty acres a man named Orcutt filed on up in

Denver."

Hyland slowly looked around and upward. Then he straightened up and drank some coffee before speaking in a level, almost amused, tone of voice. "He's mistaken, Evan."

Hatfield, too, stared at the little blue square in the expanse of the big unfolded map. It was small indeed. "Mister Hyland, he's got a patent to that land."

"You saw it?"

"Yes."

Douglas Hyland finished the coffee and put the cup down, hard. "Someone has made a mistake, maybe not Orcutt, maybe some land clerk or an agent. That's Hyland land, Evan." He stepped behind the desk, looking directly at Hatfield. "Where is this man . . . he's not over there on that land, is he?"

"No. He's back in town."

Hyland sank down, the fire crackled at his back, little fingers of raw wind scratched along the windows in the east wall, and Evan turned to resume his seat while he waited for Douglas Hyland to speak again. It was not a very long wait.

"I'll have to go through all the deeds. It'll take a day or so, but I'll find it. That's part of the original ranch my grandfather put together. That's the old part, Evan, but I've seen the deeds. Some of them are in Spanish. He traded for thousands of what they called *varas* and we call acres, not very long after he came out here." Douglas did not look angry or upset, which was a relief to the sheriff. "It's a mistake, but, until I find the deed, I don't think that man had ought to go out there."

Hatfield nodded to that; he did not think Enos Orcutt had better go out there, either. He had not thought so since Orcutt had first unfolded the map back in town. "I'll talk to him. He seems like a reasonable man."

Douglas Hyland leaned to study the map again, then he picked up a pencil and wrote what Evan assumed were descriptions of the land. When he tossed down the pencil, Hyland said: "That's impossible."

Evan agreed. "Like you said, someone made a mistake."

The cowman arose to poke a split log into the fireplace and turned back with a wag of his head. "Damned government clerks."

Evan nodded, finished his coffee,

and loosened in the chair, enjoying the heat.

Douglas Hyland went to a glass-fronted upright cabinet and brought back a bottle of whiskey. He refilled Hatfield's cup, then his own, and laced the coffee. As he went to return the bottle to the cupboard, he said: "I remember my father saying that someday there would be settlers out here. So far, though, we've seen very few."

"Back along the far foothills they've been taking up land for the past couple of years," stated the lawman. "Maybe you haven't got over there as much as I have. But they're here, all right. I'd guess we'll get a lot more. The railroads are offering reduced fares to get the business, and they dump those people out at this end of the tracks. Your pa was dead right. I think most of the cowmen own land around the free graze, though . . . the ones like yourself that have deeds . . . and that ought to keep settlers out of the valley."

Douglas Hyland returned to his desk and sat down, looked at the big map, then meticulously folded it, and tossed it aside. "I don't like to see it happen, Evan."

"Neither do I. I don't suppose anyone really likes something like this." Hatfield paused, then said: "It's caused trouble other places. I'd hate to see it start up like that around here."

Hyland nodded. "Yes. Well, this stranger, is he a range man?"

Evan, thinking of the curly-brim derby hat and button shoes, wagged his head. "Used to be a gun peddler. I don't know anything else about him except that he sure doesn't look to me like he was ever a range man."

Hyland arose, handed the sheriff the map, and said: "You'll be hungry. Let's go see what the cook's got."

As they passed through the large, elegant rooms, Evan Hatfield took a moment to envy anyone who had two generations of canny planners behind them. Then the wind rattled some windows as they passed through, and Hatfield began thinking about the long, uncomfortable ride ahead of him.

III

Sheriff Hatfield arose late and had breakfast, as he commonly did, at the café diagonally across from his jailhouse office. Because it was later than usual, he was almost the only patron of the café man. It had been a raw ride back to town last night, but this morning the sun was brilliant, the ground was firming up underfoot, and there was no vestige of that chilly wind that had prevailed last night. The café man was a former freighter whose rough existence had finally brought him to staying indoors most of the time as age and old aches caught up with him. His name was Barlow Smith. Around town they called him Barley. He was a heavyset individual who thirty years earlier had been as powerful as oak, and good-natured. He was still good-natured. He and Sheriff Hatfield had been Saturday night poker players along with several other men around town for five or six years. Now, Barley brought along a mug of java and leaned behind the counter as Hatfield ate. He said: "Damned weather in this country, a man never knows whether to put on his woolen long johns in the morning or not, and, if he don't, it'll come a cold wind sure as hell."

Evan nodded, and held forth his cup.

As Barley Smith refilled it with black coffee, he said: "Had a gunman in here this morning early who drank five cups of coffee with his steak and potatoes. Five cups. That's enough to float a flatboat."

Hatfield sipped and set the cup aside. "Raw-boned young feller with light hair and button shoes?"

"That's him. You know him?"

"No, but I met him yesterday morning."

"He had me roll up some meat in a paper to take out with him."

Evan stopped chewing and raised his eyes. "Take out where?"

"I don't know. He just said he'd need something to eat before he come back to town."

Sheriff Hatfield finished eating, downed the coffee in a pair of swallows, arose, dumped some silver on the counter top, and turned away, leaving Barley Smith looking after him in a puzzled way.

At the livery barn they confirmed

Hatfield's suspicions. A day man said: "Yeah, he hired a horse and rode out . . . hell, it must-been two hours back."

"Which way?"

The day man did not know; he'd been busy dunging out and forking feed. Hatfield said: "Fetch my horse."

As the day man went to obey, the sheriff crossed to the harness room for his outfit. After all the horsebacking he'd done yesterday, he had not anticipated repeating the experience for a while, but, hell, it was a very knowledgeable individual in this life who knew at breakfast time what he might have done by evening. Still, the horse was rested, fed, and frisky, the weather was nearly perfect, and there were advantages to being out of Hyland for a few hours.

He headed for Arapaho Creek by the most direct overland route he knew. As he rode, the irritation subsided to be replaced by uneasiness. He could not forbid Orcutt from going out there. In fact, if the man's title to that hundred and sixty acres was valid, not even Douglas Hyland could keep him off it. And, for a fact, since Lost Valley Ranch cattle were kept off this lowland range during summer so that it would be available to winter them on, there was not much chance any Hyland riders would be over there.

Evan relaxed as his horse loped over the gently undulating grassland. He had left town in a tense, troubled frame of mind, but by the time he had the willow tops in view out where the creek wandered, he was no longer tense at all, and he was only mildly troubled. The land was empty. He could see for miles in all directions, without sighting any movement, any livestock or horsemen. When he came up over the last swale with the meandering creek in front a mile or so, he saw Orcutt's livery animal standing hipshot in willow shade over where that Indian camp had been, and reined off in that direction. He did not see Orcutt until he was dismounting to tie his own horse, then the rangy man in his incongruous curly-brim derby hat and button shoes strolled out of some thickets farther along, watched Hatfield for a while, and finally ambled up to greet him with a smile.

"Good morning, Sheriff. There's no one squatting here."

Hatfield fished forth the folded map and handed it over as he said: "I didn't say anyone was, Mister Orcutt. I said folks had been using the land, meaning they'd been grazing cattle over it." As Orcutt took the map, Hatfield added: "How did you find it without the map?"

"I have another map, Sheriff." Orcutt raised his face. "Hyland claims it, doesn't he? I talked to some men at the saloon last night. This is all Hyland land, they told me, thousands and thousands of acres of it."

Evan Hatfield went to work making his first smoke of the day. "Douglas Hyland told me he has a deed to this hundred and sixty, Mister Orcutt."

"Did he show it to you?"

"No. He's going to hunt it up today." When Evan saw the rueful expression of skepticism, he added: "Mister Hyland doesn't have to lie to anyone, and he doesn't have to claim a hundred and sixty acres. He uses more land than that just for his marking ground. The reason I followed you out here is because Lost Valley Ranch has a rule about strangers wandering over Hyland land. To save all of us some headaches, it'd be better if you stayed away from here until it's settled about whose land this is."

"It's my land, Sheriff. You saw the patents they gave me in Denver."

"Uhn-huh, and Mister Hyland'll have patents, too. You see my point, Mister Orcutt?"

The raw-boned younger man stood a moment without replying, then he smiled at Evan Hatfield. "All right. Hell, a week or so isn't going to make that much difference, I guess. Not after all the years I've waited, saving up the money to do this . . . but it's my land, Sheriff."

Dryly Evan said: "Yeah. It's someone's land. One time I sat my horse right over yonder and watched some hungry Indians carve up an old cow about where we're standing. They thought it was their land, too." He dropped the cigarette and stamped on it. "Mister Orcutt, look around you. In Lost Valley it takes a hundred acres to maintain one cow. This here hundred and sixty would support one and a half cows." He wagged his head.

Orcutt smiled back. "Do you know how much potatoes sell for in town, Sheriff?"

Evan stood gazing at the younger

man. "You mean . . . farm this land?"

"What's so strange about that, Mister Hatfield? Iowa and Kansas and Nebraska and Illinois . . . that's all they do. They don't turn cattle loose to wander all over just eating the grass."

"This isn't farm land, Mister Orcutt. Look at it."

"I have looked at it. Every time I'd pass through on the stage, I'd look at it. This morning I scuffed around, dug some little holes. It's good earth, Sheriff, no rocks, and there's the creek for irrigation. Have you ever been out to California? They make ditches and carry water to their fields out there. You should see the crops they raise."

Sheriff Hatfield lifted his hat, scratched, reset the hat, and said nothing. He had seen emigrants up along the distant foothills scratching in the flinty soil up there, planting corn and beans and squash. Back in Missouri he had seen farmed land by the uninterrupted mile, but this was not farming country. This country was for cattle. Then he caught sight of far movement and turned slightly to watch a solitary horseman loping toward them.

But the rider turned northward before he saw them and went out of sight beyond the westward stretch of creek willows several miles away. It could only have been one of Douglas Hyland's men; Evan was sure of that. He turned to untie his horse as he said: "If you've seen enough, suppose we head back to town, Mister Orcutt."

Enos Orcutt watched Sheriff Hatfield untie his horse without making a move to do the same, but when Evan turned, the younger man shrugged and went toward his livery animal. He was quiet until they were riding leisurely side-by-side through the golden-lighted pleasant morning, their animals perfectly content to be heading back, then he said: "Sheriff, I'm satisfied my title to that land back yonder is valid."

Evan's retort was rueful. "And suppose it isn't?"

"It is. I'm as certain of that as I am that night will fall after supper this evening. What I wanted to say was . . . I've heard about Douglas Hyland and his riders. What I'd like you to tell me is . . . if my title is good, where will you stand?"

Evan felt annoyance stirring deep down. "Why do you think a man wears this badge? To uphold the law."

"Then you'll take my side against Mister Hyland?"

Evan leaned, expectorated, straightened up, and looked dead ahead. "I don't take sides with anyone or against anyone. My job is to maintain order and keep the peace. I'm here to make sure the law is obeyed."

"And if my title is good . . . ?"

"We'll have to wait and see, Mister Orcutt. Now let's lope these horses or we're going to miss supper."

They said very little to each other all the way back. Evan's impression was that Enos Orcutt was beginning to cool toward him. It did not bother Evan at all. He had rarely performed his duties without having someone turn sullen toward him afterward. When people were at odds and a third person came along to lay down the law, one or the other of the argumentative people ended up mad at the law. Sometimes both of them.

They reached town in mid-afternoon, went down a back alley to the livery barn. Evan Hatfield left his horse in the hands of the day man, nodded to Orcutt, and strolled in the direction of his jailhouse office. He did not notice the pair of lounging cattlemen over in the shade of the saloon overhang, but they noticed him and watched as he entered his building.

Evan pulled off his hat. He was thirsty and a little bit hungry. Sitting on a wall bench, legs crossed and relaxed, as motionless as a stone,

Douglas Hyland said: "Good afternoon, Evan."

Hatfield turned, considered the craggy features, let his breath out in a sweep, and spoke. "Good afternoon." Then he went to the dipper for a drink, and after that stepped to his desk chair, flung his hat atop the litter of papers and dodgers, and said: "I didn't expect you in town."

Hyland's blue eyes showed irony. "I didn't expect to be in town today." He paused, looking steadily across the room. "Where is this feller who has the land title?"

"I just left him at the livery barn. He rode out along the creek this morning and I went after him and brought him back."

"Is he staying at the rooming house?"

"As far as I know he is." Hatfield had a strange feeling. "Something wrong?"

Hyland faintly nodded. "You're a good man at keeping your mouth closed, Evan. I noticed that years back. I guess I have to explain something to you."

Hatfield leaned his elbows on the desk, staring. "Orcutt's title is good?"

"I want you to tell me you will not say a word about any of this."

The sheriff leaned and stared. In his mind something was sending out a tiny warning.

"Well, Evan . . . ?"

Hatfield answered slowly. "You know my position. I represent the law. I operate on the notion that there's right and wrong. The law punishes folks who kick over the traces. I can't take sides, Douglas. Don't tell me anything that's going to play hell with my job."

Hyland waited a moment before speaking, and now his voice was less rough than usual. "It's going to play hell with your job whether I tell you or not. But on the ride to town this morning I could see only one way to handle this. You have to know, otherwise it's going to be a hell of a lot harder for all of us. All I'm asking is that you keep it to yourself for a while."

Evan felt the warning more strongly than ever, but he had faith in Douglas Hyland's judgment, so he nodded. "I'll say nothing . . . but, if that has to change, I'll tell you first."

Hyland arose, crossed to the desk, and spread several very old pieces of paper on the desk top. Then he placed an equally old, yellowish, bone-dry map beside the papers. In a toneless voice he said: "Those are the Mexican deeds. That is the old Mexican map my grandfather got from the Mex officials down at Albuquerque. They had never been north of New Mexico."

Evan frowned. He did not know fifty words of Spanish and both the map and old papers were filled with it in spidery handwriting. "Can you read this stuff?" he asked.

Hyland shook his head. "Not good enough to make it all out. That's why I need time, that's why I want you to know what I'm going to do."

"You're going to find someone who can decipher it? But if those are the deeds . . . ?"

"Evan, my grandfather was not a surveyor. In his day a man swung his arm to include fifty thousand acres of land, and they signed their papers accordingly."

Evan was beginning to understand. "You mean these deeds don't take in the land along the creek Orcutt is claiming?"

Hyland leaned back. "Evan, these deeds probably do not take in twenty thousand acres, not just along the creek but north and west, too. I'd never read them before. Not until late last night after you left. I studied them all night. Evan, if they don't convey title to the Hylands for all the land between town and my home place, it won't just be the hundred and sixty acres Orcutt is claiming. Do you see what I'm faced with?"

Evan saw perfectly, and it stunned him. For three generations, since long before anyone in Lost Valley could remember, or their parents could remember, that land had been Hyland range.

Hyland quietly said: "Orcutt will only be the first." He stood looking down at Hatfield. "They'll come in here by the dozens. By the hundreds. Divide twenty thousand by a hundred and sixty, and that's how many emigrants we'll have arriving in Hyland. It's not just Lost Valley Ranch. If they come here like that, they'll outnumber us all to hell. That means they'll be after the free-graze land the other cow outfits don't have title to, but which they surround with deeded land."

Hyland began carefully to fold his

papers. He pocketed them and returned to the wall bench. "No cowman I know, Evan, is going to sit on his butt and watch something like that happen." Hyland waited until Sheriff Hatfield had digested all this and was leaning back off the desk, then Hyland also said: "That's why I need you to keep this in strict confidence until I can get back from Albuquerque, then go up to Denver as well."

Evan groped for his makings and lowered his head to roll the cigarette he felt no need for. When he'd lighted up, he looked at Douglas Hyland. "How in the hell didn't someone in your family figure this out before?"

"My grandfather spoke Spanish. Neither my father nor I had any reason to learn it. But in school back

East I had a little of it. In my grand-father's day there were lots of Mex traders and stockmen in Colorado, and even Wyoming and Montana. My father evidently did as I've done . . . assumed the Mexican deeds were correct."

"How long is it going to take you to get this figured out?"

Hyland arose tiredly. "I don't know. But I'll leave for Albuquerque in the morning. Maybe a couple of weeks, maybe a month."

IV

The following morning Evan Hatfield sat at the café counter thoughtfully drinking coffee, while around him the other single men who lived in town noisily talked and ate. Hatfield was in a troubled world of his own and the roof could have fallen in without his noticing it.

Later, he was in the office across the road when Steve Clampitt, the general store proprietor, walked in with the morning mail, placed it atop the desk, and said: "Beautiful day, Evan."

Hatfield looked up. He hadn't noticed. "Got time for a cup of coffee?"

Clampitt had the time and sat down as the sheriff filled two cups over by the wood stove and turned with them as he said: "How's business?"

"Good," stated the wiry, graying storekeeper, and grinned. "How's business with you?"

Evan grinned back. "Not so good, and that's the way I like it."

Clampitt tasted the coffee. "I'm getting calls for things I never stocked much before. Plows and harrows and such like. Those settlers up along the far hills are taking hold. Like everyone else around town, I thought they'd starve out the first winter."

Evan returned to the desk chair. "A lot of them do, Steve. The last time I was up through there I saw abandoned hovels one after another."

Clampitt had an observation to offer about that. "They tell me as fast as one leaves the country, another one comes along to take his place. And there's some good comes of it. I been offered bushels of beans and corn, even fresh vegetables. It expands my trade, handling stuff like that." Clampitt leaned back to get comfortable in the chair. "I don't give 'em credit, and that slows them down a lot. Mostly they got no money. But we trade a lot." He finished the coffee but did not stir from the chair. "I've heard talk that they're going to come down closer to town." Clampitt looked steadily at the sheriff. "I don't see how, with all the land already taken up down here, but I keep hearing that talk."

"Who from, the settlers?"

"Not so much from them. From freighters mostly. They pass through those shanty town settlements up there and pick up all the gossip." Clampitt smiled again. "The best source of information is a freighter. He knows more'n most newspapers. I tell you, Evan, we're in a period of change."

Hatfield's coffee tasted bitter to

him. "I hope not, Steve. I don't see too much wrong with things as they are."

Clampitt finally arose. "Well, one thing about change . . . it usually means growth, and stores like mine do a lot better." He thanked Evan for the coffee and departed, leaving the sheriff gazing at the door for a moment, before turning his attention to the mail.

It was not very interesting. It rarely was. Among the letters were four envelopes with Wanted posters enclosed, which he studied, then filed in a cardboard box in a corner he kept for that purpose. Otherwise, there was a letter from a wife back in Kansas whose man had deserted her and she thought he might be in Colorado. Along with this letter was a description of the wayward husband. It could have fitted two-thirds of the men Evan Hatfield saw every day.

The final letter was from the Southern Pacific Railroad Company with an enclosed map showing railroad land in alternating sections so that Sheriff Hatfield would be knowledgeable when settlers came around to enquire where specific parcels of land were. None of those square miles of land — six hundred and forty acres — was within fifty miles of Hyland and most of them were more than a hundred miles distant. The letter was obviously one of thousands printed for transmittal to town authorities throughout the entire territory up as far as the Canadian line. Hatfield sat studying it until Enos Orcutt walked in, then he shoved the map aside and leaned back to say: "Good morning."

Orcutt was no longer wearing his two-button coat, little curly-brimmed hat, and button shoes. He looked quite different in a range man's butternut shirt, cowhide boots, and broad-brimmed hat. He laughed at Sheriff Hatfield's expression and sounded a little self-conscious as he said — "The only thing that doesn't feel right is the gun." — and took the chair Steve Clampitt had relinquished an hour back.

Hatfield gazed at the ivory-butted Colt. It was nickel-plated; rarely did anyone show up in town with a gun like that, and in fact it was a matter of scornful amusement among range riders when they encountered someone wearing such a weapon.

"Fancy," he told Orcutt.

The lanky man agreed. "Not exactly ordinary, for a fact, Sheriff, but it's one of the demonstrators I used when I was peddling them. I have two more, one silver-inlaid, and the other gold-plated."

Hatfield winced. "Don't wear 'em on Saturday night at the saloon," he said good-naturedly, and they both laughed. Then Orcutt settled back in the chair, his smile gone.

"I heard around town that Mister Hyland was here last evening."

Hatfield nodded. "Yeah."

"You talked with him?"

"Yes, we talked."

"Is that all, Sheriff?"

Evan shifted slightly in the chair. "No, that's not all. He asked about you and I told him as much as I knew."

"What did he say about my land?"

"Well, Mister Orcutt, he brought me his deeds, if that's what you're here about. They seemed all right to me, but I'm no land agent."

"Sheriff, I can't believe the people over in Denver don't know their jobs. I keep thinking about this, and I keep coming back to that. They had big maps and legal descriptions. They deal in land all day long."

"There never was a man born, Mister Orcutt, who couldn't be mistaken. That goes for government people as well as anyone else. But one way or the other, my situation is pretty obvious to me . . . keep you from antagonizing Lost Valley Ranch, and keep them from burying you."

"What am I supposed to do, then . . . sit here in Hyland twiddling my thumbs?"

"You said it yourself . . . another week or so isn't going to make all that much difference."

Orcutt slumped in the chair. "Yes, I said it. But summer's moving right along. I'd like to get a cabin up before winter."

Evan Hatfield gazed pensively at the younger man. "You got a team and wagon?"

"No."

"Mister Orcutt, the nearest timber of house logs is sixty miles northeast, to the mountains. That's three days going out, empty, and five days coming back with a load. And you got to make maybe six, eight trips just to get four walls up for a small house. Then comes the roof, and, if you'd begun last spring, you just maybe could have got it done. This late in the season all you'll be able to do is stockpile the logs and wait until next spring to draw-knife the bark off 'em and start putting them up. And you don't even have a team and wagon."

Orcutt said: "How about a soddy?"

Hatfield sighed. "Next to a creek, Mister Orcutt? I know they build them up in the foothills. I've seen settler soddies up there, but that's high ground. Even so there's nothing less healthful than wintering in a house dug out of the ground. Even in high country they drip water after the first big snow and don't dry out until midsummer. But you dig a soddy hole over in the breaks along Arapaho Creek, Mister Orcutt, and you'll be up to your ankles in water all winter long."

The younger man sat gazing across the room at Hatfield. "You're for the Hyland interests, aren't you, Sheriff?"

Hatfield waited a moment before speaking. "I'll let that pass. I told you on the ride back to town I'm for the law."

"Everything I say you scuttle for me."

"Mister Orcutt, maybe that's because I've been out here a long time. I've seen it all happen many times. If you don't want to hear it from me, hire a horse, ride up to the foothills, and visit those shanty towns up there. Ask those folks."

Orcutt was momentarily silent before saying: "Last night I walked out east of town to a wagon camp and had supper with some folks from Pennsylvania."

Hatfield nodded. There were always wagoners passing through. Ever since he'd been in Hyland they'd come straggling along, and had continued to straggle along, usually bound for Oregon.

"They got some maps in Denver, too."

Hatfield's gaze narrowed almost imperceptibly. "Of this country?"

"Yes, there are four adults. They're filed on four hundred-and-sixty-acre parcels. They've got deeds to a full section of Arapaho Creek land."

Hatfield waited a moment, then went digging for his makings. As he worked up a smoke, he said — "One square mile." — and the younger man nodded. As the sheriff lit up, he shook his head. "Hell."

Orcutt, watching Hatfield, repeated

what he'd said earlier. "You don't like to see the cattle interests challenged, do you?"

This time, Evan Hatfield's temper slipped a notch. "I don't like to see people buried. I don't like to see them get burned out and shot up."

Orcutt had evidently arrived at the jailhouse office with this kind of confrontation in mind, because now he said: "We discussed that last night at the wagon camp. I told them about my experience. They're going to stand up for their rights."

Evan growled back. "Rights, my butt. Even if they've got 'em, Mister Orcutt, I've yet to see a piece of land I'd want to get shot over."

"That's your job, Sheriff . . . to make sure folks who got rights are protected."

Now Evan's anger was simmering very close to the surface. "You've traveled the country, Mister Orcutt. You know there are cattlemen grazing over every mile of it. Do you think one lawman can be everywhere?"

"Lawmen can raise posses, Sheriff."

"You greener'n I thought. Sure I can raise posses. I do it every now and then to chase down rustlers and horse thieves. Every cow outfit gives me men when I need 'em, and every house here in Hyland has guns in it, men who know how to use them, and folks who are willing to help when I need it against outlaws." Evan leaned across the desk. "I couldn't raise five men to protect squatters from cattlemen. Not five, Mister Orcutt."

"Last night around the fire one of

those Pennsylvanians said they'd called in the Army over east of here in the Nebraska hills country when this sort of thing came up."

Evan arose, got himself a cup of coffee, refilled another cup, and handed it to Enos Orcutt, then went back to his chair. "The nearest Army post, Mister Orcutt, is up at Fort Laramie in Wyoming. Do you know how far that is from Hyland?"

Orcutt knew. "I've been through there many times, Sheriff. I know how far it is. We can wait."

Evan sighed. "Then do it. Wait right here in town, but don't go setting up any camps along Arapaho Creek."

"You don't have the authority to forbid us from. . . ."

"God damn it, Mister Orcutt, I'm not forbidding you from doing anything. I'm just trying to keep the peace. By now you've talked to enough folks around town to know that Lost Valley Ranch is death on trespassers. I'm trying to keep you and them apart. I thought I made that plain to you." Evan gulped coffee and shoved the cup aside. "What's a week or two? You said that yourself. What's the name of those folks you visited with last night?"

"Schmidt and Langer. Why, are you going out there?"

Evan nodded. "I'll go talk to them."

Orcutt looked doubtful and Hatfield saw the look. "Sheriff, I doubt that you'll have much luck."

Evan shrugged thick shoulders.

"Do you want me to ride along with you?"

Evan thought about that, and almost decided against it. "Seems to me you got them stirred up last night. I don't need that kind of help when I'm talking to them."

"I didn't stir them up. Well, I didn't do it on purpose. I told them what's happened to me around here, and what I think the trouble is."

"Sure you did. Me. I'm the trouble."

Enos Orcutt drained his cup before speaking again. "The trouble is, Sheriff, three generations of a family named Hyland have been riding roughshod over free-graze land. Hyland, and the other cowmen in Lost Valley."

"And that's not stirring them up?" said Evan, arising from behind his desk. "You stay here in town." He went to the wall rack, took down a booted carbine, slung it carelessly over a shoulder, and went back to get his hat at the desk. "Mister Orcutt, we've talked about this until hell's half froze over. What it boils down to is simply this . . . stay off Hyland range for a couple more weeks. It may inconvenience you, but that's a hell of a lot better than getting shot or whipped raw. It'd be better to have to put off building your cabin until next spring, than not to be around to build it at all."

Hatfield opened the door, held it open until his guest walked out ahead of him, then closed it. He nodded and turned southward in the direction of the livery barn, mad all the way through.

Behind him, Orcutt stood as though he were undecided, watching the

larger, older man's progress, then Orcutt crossed toward the general store.

It was not quite midday. There was
a pleasant layer of heat over the
world, not a breath of wind from any
direction, and at the livery barn,
when Sheriff Hatfield growled for his
horse, the liveryman looked startled,
not just at Hatfield's flinty look and
growl, but because Hatfield had that
booted Winchester slung over his
shoulder.

V

East of Hyland, where the creek ran
diagonally across miles of grazed-over
grassland, there were about a dozen
places where emigrants passing
through, and freighters, set up camps.

Most of those places had been used so much they had permanent stone rings for cooking and limbless trees for tethering livestock. Sheriff Hatfield had no difficulty finding the camp he was looking for. It consisted of two battered, sturdy old wagons, a dozen horses hobbled nearby down along the creek where the grass was best, and smoke still rising from breakfast fires.

There were four children hunting bird nests along the lower creek who saw Hatfield approaching, and fled like quail back to the camp, and by the time Hatfield got up there two men were waiting, and behind them, hovering over near the wagons, two women and the children were motionlessly watching.

Evan rode up, halted, and soberly

nodded. The men nodded back just as soberly, then one, a bull-necked, nearly square man with unshorn sun-bleached hair motioned toward the fire ring. "Get down, Sheriff. We got hot coffee."

Evan dismounted, hobbled his animal, and went to the stone ring. The other man was taller, but he, too, was powerfully put together. He offered a big hand and said: "Otto Langer. This is Henry Schmidt, Sheriff." Then Langer went for the tin cups to pour coffee.

Evan considered the wagons, the peering women, then turned farther to look at the livestock. Mostly, settlers had poor, overworked horses. These people had good big strong young animals in fair flesh. Their camp was orderly, the way camps commonly were among people who had been living on the ground for a long time. He faced the men, who were waiting, watching him closely. Neither man was armed. They wore the thick, flat-heeled boots of drovers, and wore suspenders instead of belts. Their hats, too, were different, but their faces showed the sun squint, the bronze shadings, of all people who faced into the sun most of every day, and that included range men.

Evan tasted the coffee. It was strong enough to float a horseshoe, but he smiled a little and said: "Thanks. It's fine coffee."

Neither of the men spoke.

Evan shifted his stance a little, then spoke bluntly. "You folks got maps of the land around here, and you got deeds to some land over on Arapaho

Creek. A young feller named Orcutt told me that this morning. What I rode out to tell you is that the title to that land lies with a man named Douglas Hyland."

The shorter, bull-necked man said bleakly: "We know who he is."

The man's tone made Sheriff Hatfield gaze steadily at him as he resumed speaking. "Mister Schmidt, my position is to keep the peace. I'll ask you folks the same thing I asked Mister Orcutt . . . stay off Hyland's range for a couple of weeks. Until it can be figured out whether the men at the Land Office in Denver made a mistake about that land, or not."

The taller man, Otto Langer, said: "Sheriff, we got families. It's hard enough in summertime but in winter. . . ." He wagged his head. "We got to get shelters built before snow flies."

Evan leaned gently to put the tin cup upon one of the stones at his feet. As he straightened up, he said: "If you build shelters on someone else's land, Mister Langer, they'll tear them down."

"It isn't someone else's land," stated Henry Schmidt. "Do you want to see the patents they gave us in Denver?"

"No. I'm satisfied you got them, Mister Schmidt. But I'm not satisfied they're valid."

Otto Langer looked intently at Hatfield. "You a cowman, Sheriff?"

"No, I'm a lawman."

"But you worked for cowmen some time, Sheriff. This Douglas Hyland is a friend of yours?"

Evan could feel the color coming

into his face. "Gents, let's get this out of the way right now. No matter who my friends are . . . or aren't . . . I administer the law. It's got not a damned thing to do with who my friends are. Now, let's get back to this other matter."

"First," stated Langer, shoving big hands into trouser pockets, "let me tell you that in Denver, when we asked if anyone else might be using our land, they told us we had a right to get the law out here to run them off. That's your job, isn't it?"

"If it is your land, Mister Langer. *If.*"

Schmidt jutted his heavy jaw. "We got the deeds to prove it."

"So does Mister Hyland!"

"His aren't any good."

Evan bit back his angry retort,

paused, then in a calmer voice said: "Gents, he thinks different. What we're talking about right now isn't who owns the land. What we're talking about is . . . until it's settled whose title is right and proper you folks keep off Arapaho Creek. Stay plumb away."

Schmidt was red in the face when he sourly said: "Sure, we keep off our own land so that damned cowman can graze off all the grass we'll need for our horses this winter. We keep off it until winter, then it'll be too late to build cabins and we'll either starve or freeze, maybe both. You see those children over yonder?"

Evan held himself in check with an effort. He did not look toward the wagons, he looked directly at Henry Schmidt. "None of this is my doing,

Mister Schmidt. I know it's going to inconvenience the hell out of you, but if you go over there and set up a camp, Hyland's riders will visit you, and that's not going to happen if I can prevent it. Any way you look at it, gents, this is a hell of a mess, and, if you think it's only bad for you, you're wrong. It's just as bad for me."

Henry Schmidt did not give an inch. "How bad for you? You got a stove in your office in town? You got a dry bed every night, Sheriff, and . . . ?"

Hatfield had had enough. With a hand resting on his gun butt he said: "I'm not going to repeat it. Keep away from Arapaho Creek for the next two weeks." He waited, but neither of the men across the stone ring from him spoke. They looked steadily at him, though, without a hint of irresolution, as he thanked them for the coffee, removed the hobbles from his horse, swung up, and turned stiffly in the direction of town.

The best he could do was be hopeful, and, as he got close to Hyland's outskirts with his red mood diminishing, he thought Otto Langer might be reasonable. He did not believe he had made a favorable impression out there, and was disappointed about that. As for Henry Schmidt, he knew that type of man. Schmidt would probably never yield at all. If he did, he would never do it gracefully.

At the livery barn, Evan unbuckled the booted Winchester, left his horse with a hostler, and returned to the office. He was re-racking the saddle gun when Joe Lamont walked in, tugging off his riders' gloves. Joe said: " 'Afternoon, Sheriff. You got a few minutes to spare?"

Evan nodded and gestured toward a chair. As Lamont sat down and tucked the gloves under his gun belt, Hatfield said: "Did Mister Hyland get off all right?"

Lamont thumbed back his hat. "Yeah, he got off. He didn't tell me a hell of a lot, but I've worked for him a long time, and he was worried."

Evan thought that Douglas Hyland had reason to be worried, and sat behind the old flat-top desk. "Things'll work out, Joe, they always do."

The dark-eyed, graying range boss agreed. "Yeah, they always do." Then he sat a moment, probably organizing what he'd come here to say. "We're gettin' some trespassers over along the creek. It don't amount to much, I guess, except that Mister Hyland told me before he left not to let anyone hang around over there."

"Have you seen 'em, Joe?"

"No. We don't ride that part of the ranch very much, until we bring in the cattle for wintering. But there are some tracks, and I expect now I'll have to keep someone over there watching, and right now I sure can't spare the rider nor the time." Lamont's dark eyes came up. "I was wondering, Sheriff . . . if you was to be out there once in a while, if you'd sort of keep an eye peeled?"

Evan nodded because he had made up his mind on the ride back from the settler camp to do this. "Yeah.

And there's something you can do for me, Joe."

"Sure. Shoot."

"If you find anyone over there, don't get all fired up. Don't let your men get fired up. I guess Mister Hyland told you about settlers coming around."

"He said something about a feller named Orcutt."

"There are two more, along with Orcutt. One's named Langer, and the other one's named Schmidt."

Joe Lamont gazed at Hatfield. "Settlers . . . three settlers bothering over along the creek? They think they got a right over there?"

"Yeah, they think so."

Joe Lamont kept gazing at Hatfield, then he abruptly stood up. "Maybe you'd ought to tell them not to go over there, Sheriff."

Evan also arose. "I've already told them, Joe. Now remember . . . if your men see someone out there, don't start something."

Lamont went to the door before replying to that. He frowned a little at Sheriff Hatfield. "When Mister Hyland's gone, I look after things for him, and that includes running off folks who got no business on the range."

He went out and closed the door after himself. He had not agreed to leave trespassers to the sheriff, and Evan stood at the desk remembering the look in Joe Lamont's dark eyes.

"Hell," he growled at the wall, and went over to dip up a drink of water before going out to make a round of the town.

He ended up at the café and Barley Smith brought him roast beef, tough enough to cover a saddle tree with, which was the way Hatfield liked his roasts, and some apple pie made from pithy little stone-sized crab apples that had to be sweetened with their own weight in sugar, and still they were tart.

Barley related an incident that had occurred out front of Clampitt's store earlier in the day, and looked intently at Sheriff Hatfield as he mentioned it.

"That lanky gunman I told you about for drinking five cups of coffee. Well, by golly, he was coming out of the store this afternoon and one of Hyland's men was standing there in the shade, and said something. I don't know what, because I wasn't that close, but I tell you, Evan, that raw-boned feller in his new clothes and all . . . for a fact he sure did look green."

Hatfield listened. "Go on."

"Well, sir, the gunman made a remark back and that cowboy stepped off the boards into the dust and called the gunman a son-of-a-bitch."

Hatfield did not move. "And . . . ?"

"Evan, you never in your life saw a man with a draw like that. Button shoes and derby hat or not, I never saw anything like it, and neither have you. He had that shiny gun out and cocked, and aimed dead center on that cowboy's breast bone, before the cowboy had even cleared his holster. Then he says . . . 'You unbuckle that gun belt, let it drop, toss down the gun, and go out into the middle of the road and start walking, and, mister, when you're ready to apologize, come on back and I'll return the gun and shell belt.' And by golly that range man did it, hiking south to the livery barn without once looking back. Evan, I tell you, if that man's not a gunfighter, I'll eat my boots."

Hatfield shoved the pie away, swallowed a few more mouthfuls of tough roast beef, then paid up, and walked out of the café.

The day was ending; shadows slanted from building fronts across the way. The sun was masked by an afternoon heat haze that was lying far out. As Sheriff Hatfield turned in the direction of the rooming house, the evening stage arrived early, which was unusual, in fact for a stage even to arrive on time was unusual but,

for one to reach town ahead of sched-
ule brought a lot of heads around.

VI

By the time Sheriff Hatfield located
Enos Orcutt there were shadows
along the verandah of the rooming
house, and out the front door came
the smell of greasy cooking. There
were only two other men on the
porch, and, after the sheriff's arrival,
they decided to cross to the saloon
for a drink before supper. As they
trudged away, one said: "Likely need
more'n just one drink to screw up my
nerve to eat supper in there again
tonight."

For a fact the rooming house proprietor and his wife set forth the

worst meals anywhere in Lost Valley, and it might even have been as traveling men had suggested — that they served meals like that to discourage roomers from eating at the establishment. Sheriff Hatfield resided at the rooming house, and had not so much as entered the dining room there for five years.

Tonight, he went over where Orcutt was sitting, long legs raised, feet hooked over the verandah railing, dragged around a chair, and sat down as he said: "Nice night, isn't it?"

Orcutt turned slightly. "Very nice night. I'll guess why you're here, Mister Hatfield. That fracas out front of the store."

Evan liked directness. "I want the six-gun and shell belt, Mister Orcutt, and I want to tell you again . . . one more time . . . what can happen to folks who lock horns with Lost Valley Ranch."

Orcutt did not allow Hatfield the opportunity to explain what could happen. He shot up to his feet, murmured something about the shell belt and gun, and disappeared inside.

Hatfield rolled a smoke, watched them close the log gates of the corral yard southward, and speculated upon the identity of four range men who walked their horses toward the saloon tie rack, and by then the settler returned and handed over to the sheriff what obviously was someone else's holstered Colt and shell belt.

"It wasn't my doing," he said. "I was coming out of the store. There was a range man leaning there. He said . . . 'Mister, if you ain't careful someone'll take that shiny pistol and ram it. . . .' "

"I heard what happened, Mister Orcutt. He called you a son-of-a-bitch."

"Not until after I told him no one as ugly and smelly as he was would take my gun. Then he called me that and stepped off the duckboards."

"And you outdrew him."

"Sheriff, gun peddlers only sell pistols if they can show how to use them. Draw faster than anyone else. Every town I've ever been in has got someone they figure is fast and accurate. Gun peddlers have got to beat that kind of competition wherever they go. Otherwise, they don't peddle guns."

Hatfield knew all this. He'd been marveling at the dead-shot, fast-draw gun peddlers since he'd been a boy. "Did you know that was a Hyland rider?"

Orcutt strung both long legs over the railing as he resumed his former position again. "Not right then I didn't. That man who runs the café told me afterward who the rider was."

"When he gets back to the ranch, he'll tell 'em. Tomorrow they'll be in town looking for you. Maybe even tonight."

"I can handle it, Sheriff."

"No you can't, Mister Orcutt, and, even if you could, you're not going to try it . . . not in my town." Sheriff Hatfield turned. "Starting tomorrow, you go unarmed."

Orcutt stared.

"That's right, unarmed, Mister Orcutt, because around Lost Valley they don't shoot unarmed men. But you show up in the roadway tomorrow when Lost Valley Ranch is in town, and I don't care how fast you are, you can't make it against nine men. Now then, either I get your word about this tonight, or I'll waltz you down to the jailhouse right now, and keep you locked up for a spell."

Orcutt was aghast. "For what? All I did was protect myself against a damned bully. That's all."

"All right, Mister Orcutt, I'll accept that," stated Evan Hatfield. "Now then, you going to pass me your word or not?"

"Sheriff, the man was standing there to pick a fight."

Hatfield leaned, and Orcutt got a strange look on his face as something round and unyieldingly hard was pressed into his rib cage on the left side. "Stand up, Mister Orcutt. Stand up!"

As the raw-boned younger man arose that pair of roomers came back across the road from the saloon, ignored the pair of standing men farther along the verandah in the gloom, and went reluctantly inside.

Enos Orcutt felt Hatfield's big hand on his arm as the sheriff turned him a little, then leaned and lifted away his nickel-plated six-gun. As he straightened up, Hatfield shoved hard with his pistol barrel. "Walk. Not a damned word out of you, just walk down to the jailhouse. If you get clever and try ducking between a couple of buildings, I'll aim low and break a leg."

"Sheriff. . . ."

"I said not a damned word. Walk!"

A great many people around Lost Valley could have told Enos Orcutt this was exactly how Evan Hatfield operated. When he decided to move, he did not waste any time and he did not use one superfluous word. And he was fast, even in broad daylight Hatfield was fast and accurate with his six-gun.

Orcutt trudged toward the jailhouse as silent as a mute. When Hatfield opened the door, shoved him through it, and lighted a lamp, Orcutt finally spoke.

"Sheriff, I was absolutely justified in what I did. Any man would have done the same, except that most of them would have shot and killed that cowboy. I could have, but I didn't."

Evan motioned. "Shuck the shell belt."

It was like trying to reason with a stone wall. Orcutt let the bullet belt drop, and obeyed when Hatfield gestured him down the little corridor into one of the strap-steel cages in the jailhouse cell room. Only after he had Enos Orcutt locked in did the sheriff relax. He stood out front and said: "It wasn't just the business with the Hyland range rider. I talked to Langer and Schmidt. They had their backs up when I rode up. Mister Orcutt, I'll fill these damned cells if I have to. Yeah, I know what you're going to say . . . it was justified. I believe you." Orcutt stared, and Hatfield smiled at him before continuing: "I try to make sense to you people, and don't make a dent. For the last time I'll tell you . . . it's not title to that damned land along the creek that worries me, it's keeping a war from starting."

He turned on his heel and went back to the office, drew down the lamp, and for the first time in months, when he returned to the plank walk out front, Hatfield locked his jailhouse door. It did not occur to him that his prisoner hadn't had supper. He could not have done much about it if it had, because the café across the road was dark.

Ordinarily he would have headed for his room, but after the episode with Orcutt he was wide awake, so he stopped by the saloon for a nightcap, and ran into Joe Lamont with two Lost Valley Ranch range men, none of whom looked at Sheriff Hatfield with the easy amiability that had for years marked the association between Douglas Hyland's men and the local law. Hatfield nodded without smiling and stepped up along the bar for his drink. Until it arrived, Lamont remained in his place with his men, dourly pensive. But after Hatfield had downed his shot of whiskey, Joe came down and leaned beside the sheriff.

"Those tracks goin' up along Arapaho Creek," he said, by way of openers. "Maybe they was made by that Orcutt feller, Sheriff."

Hatfield nodded. He knew what was coming.

"Today he jumped Arthur Daggett out front of the store here in town."

Evan shifted position, rested his stomach against the bar, and negatively shook his head when the barman came along to raise an enquiring eyebrow. As the barman departed, Hatfield said: "I think it happened the other way around, Joe. I think your man pushed that gunman into a fight. And, Joe, from what I've heard from folks who saw it, your man is lucky he's alive." Evan looked straight at the range boss. "I've got your man's gun and belt over on my desk. He can come claim 'em the next time he's in town."

Lamont's dark eyes were hard. "He'll be along. That gunman made him look bad, walkin' down the road like he done."

Evan shrugged. "He can come any time. But all he's going to get is his gun back. I've got the gunman locked in a cell."

Lamont's expression changed slowly. "Well, by golly, I'm glad to hear that, Sheriff."

Hatfield forced a small smile. He could have explained that the reason he had locked up Orcutt had nothing to do with the gun action out front of the general store that day, but he didn't do it. Lamont could believe anything he wanted to believe, and, if it happened to be that Sheriff Hatfield was sympathetic to the cattle interests, that was all right with Hatfield. All he wanted was — no trouble.

He left Lamont standing there, returned to the chilly late evening, and went on up to his room. He was tired, and he hadn't actually done anything to make him that way. He dozed off thinking of what those emigrants had said about needing feed for their livestock and shelter for their broods. In the morning he awakened thinking of Joe Lamont's misinterpretation concerning the incarceration of Enos Orcutt.

Evidently the news had spread. Barley Smith waited until Hatfield was nearly finished with his breakfast, then he asked if Evan wanted a pail of coffee and some beef stew to take across the road with him. Evan nodded, expecting more, but Barley Smith was a discreet individual. He padded to his kitchen to fill the little pails and returned to stand them upon his counter, without once mentioning how he knew there was a prisoner in one of the cells across the road. If Barley Smith knew, then so did everyone else around town, not that it was a secret, but it intrigued Hatfield how the information had got around so swiftly.

He shoved the pails under Orcutt's cell door and was agreeable when the prisoner asked if he could wash after he ate. Hatfield went out to the office to pour fresh water into the coffee pot atop his wood stove, fling in another fistful of ground beans, and was stuffing kindling into the stove when a woman walked in from the roadway. He looked owlishly at her. The number of females who had visited his jailhouse over the years he could have counted on the fingers of one hand.

She acted as self-conscious about being there as Hatfield felt about having her there. He got a chair for her and murmured something about the coffee being ready in a little while, and tried hard to remember where he had seen her before.

She dispelled the mystery. "Sheriff, I'm Missus Langer. I saw you at our camp yesterday."

Hatfield sighed, and went around to his desk chair to sit down. She was a tall woman, well put together, with wavy dark brown hair and eyes that matched. He would have guessed her age to be close to his own, and would have missed by five years; she was just barely thirty.

She blurted out the first words with both hands clasped in her lap. "I'm afraid, Sheriff."

To make it easier for her Evan smiled. "I am, too, ma'am, but with any luck at all nothing is going to happen."

She lowered her eyes to the clasped hands. "Last night another wagon arrived."

Hatfield's smile dwindled. "Settlers?"

"Yes. A family from Kentucky named Horne. Mister Horne, his wife, and their two half-grown boys."

Evan eased back in his chair. He could guess the rest of it. "You folks visited with them?"

Langer's wife kept looking down. "Yes. Last night and again this morning. Last night the men brought out a jug and talked long after Missus Schmidt and I put the youngsters to bed."

"This Mister Horne . . . how did he impress you, ma'am?"

"That's what worries me, Sheriff. He's a Southerner, a hard-fisted man with strong opinions. My husband . . . after you rode away yesterday, my husband told Henry Schmidt there didn't seem to be much else to do but wait the two weeks you mentioned. Henry is a little like Mister Horne . . . he's impatient and. . . ."

"Willing to be a little troublesome?"

"Well, he's right, Sheriff. We have to build shelters before winter. But as I told my husband . . . this whole country is populated by people who will oppose us, and we're only two families." She finally looked up. Her face was pale and her eyes seemed darker as a result of that. "I told my husband this morning I'd rather go on, keep going until we got to Oregon even, because I was afraid. He said all we had to do was wait, there would be more emigrants arriving soon, then the cowmen wouldn't be able to bully us."

Evan went to the stove to poke in another couple of pieces of wood. When he turned back, the handsome tall woman was standing. He said: "This will be between us, Missus Langer. And I'm right obliged you came."

"Can you do anything to stop it before it starts, Sheriff?"

Evan's answer was quietly offered, but strong. "That's my plan. Whether your husband and Mister Schmidt believed me yesterday, or not, when I told them all I wanted was to make sure there was no trouble, it is the absolute truth." He went to the door with her and opened it. "Again, ma'am, I'm obliged to you."

After she had departed, Hatfield

went over to sniff the coffee pot. The brew was not quite hot yet, but he drew off a cup anyway. It tasted terrible, but maybe that had less to do with the coffee than it had to do with the way Hatfield was feeling right then.

VII

The morning stage arrived an hour and a half late, which could have been important to the men who operated the company's corral yard, but not to anyone else around town. An aftereffect was that the mail was not sifted and sorted into its little cubicles over at the general store until about noon.

When Sheriff Hatfield strolled over,

Steve Clampitt got his three letters, passed them over, and leaned in a conspiratorial manner to say softly: "Had three settlers in here this morning."

Evan nodded without much interest as he looked at his three letters.

"They bought bullets for handguns, some shells for shotguns, and two boxes of Winchester ammunition."

Evan looked up and Clampitt grinned bleakly across the counter at him.

Later, when Hatfield was out back at the wash rack with Enos Orcutt, he mentioned the newcomer, Horne, and Orcutt spoke from a face dripping with cold water. "Sheriff, there's bound to be more. They got big maps on the walls at the Denver Land Office showing all this country, and with the parcels in blue which can be homesteaded." As he reached for the grimy old towel, he also said: "You can't any more stop progress than you can fly, Mister Hatfield."

Evan grunted. "You think growth is progress, Mister Orcutt? I don't." He herded his prisoner back to the office, motioned for him to sit along the wall, and got them both cups of coffee. When he was handing a cup to the lanky settler, he said: "Two weeks isn't ten years."

Orcutt agreed. "I was willing to stay in town and wait it out. Sheriff, I don't think the cattlemen will wait. Why else did that range man try to start a fight with me across the road?"

"They'll wait," stated Hatfield in a growling tone.

"Tell me, Sheriff . . . did someone

go up to Denver? Is that why all this waiting is important?"

"To Denver, yes, but down to Albuquerque first." Hatfield did not elaborate. He would not have explained even if Orcutt had asked him to. But Orcutt did not ask. He instead made a statement.

"I doubt that it'll turn out the way you hope, Sheriff."

Hatfield did not comment. If Orcutt was right, then the headaches were only just beginning for Hatfield, and he had known this since the day he'd last spoken with Douglas Hyland. "Finish your coffee," he said, and, when Orcutt put the cup aside and was herded back down into the cell room, he waited to speak until Hatfield had locked him in again.

"What about Schmidt and Langer?"

Hatfield pocketed the key. "They're unhappy. You knew that. Now, there's this other one, a feller named Horne who just pulled in yesterday."

Orcutt said: "I told you. And there'll be more."

Hatfield returned to the office, closed the damper on his wood stove, picked up his hat, and went out into the warming new day sunlight. A solitary rider was coming down past the rooming house from the north. Hatfield only recognized him when the rider turned in toward the jailhouse tie rack. It was the range man Orcutt had disarmed, Art Daggett, and, as he dismounted to tie up, he shot Hatfield an unsmiling look.

"Joe said you got my gun and belt, Sheriff."

Hatfield reached back, opened the

jailhouse door, and led the way inside to his desk. As he picked up the holstered Colt and held it forth, he said: "Don't try that again."

The cowboy flung his shell belt around, caught the buckle, and made it fast. Then he hefted the weapon and looked straight at Sheriff Hatfield. "I guess I can't. Joe says you got that greenhorn locked up."

"He won't be locked up forever," stated the lawman, "and, when he comes out . . . he'll kill you if you try it again."

Daggett seemed about to speak, checked the impulse, and turned toward the door. "Thanks," he said, and walked out to his horse.

For the second time Hatfield returned to the roadway. Arthur Daggett was riding southward at a walk, down to the lower end of town, and on out. He did not cut westward the way a rider would have done who was going back to Lost Valley Ranch, and Hatfield briefly speculated about that, but had his ruminations interrupted by a red-faced, lanky man who was driving a wagon in from east of town, making enough noise to have been a herd of wagons. The sideboards rattled, the wheels ground over dry axles, and the tailgate chain was so loose it spanked wood with every chuck hole.

The red-faced man turned northward into the main road and saw Hatfield watching, sang out to his horses, kicked on the brake, and leaned to spray amber before calling over: "Which way to the buggy works, friend?"

Hyland did not have a wagon works, but it had a smithy where local wagon work was done and Hatfield pointed. "Yonder, that open gate south of the corral yard." As he dropped his arm, he saw the staring look the red-faced man was giving him. The man had evidently not noticed Evan's badge when he had first accosted him. Now, straightening on the wagon seat, the stranger showed clear, candid hostility as he nodded, yanked loose the brake, and started up his team. He turned once, a few yards ahead, and stared back.

Hatfield speculated that this might be Horne, the newly arrived settler. What made him inclined to believe it was the red-faced man's accent. He was a Southerner; he might not have been that particular Southerner, but he certainly had the drawl of the South.

Joe Lamont arrived in town from Lost Valley Ranch about the time Evan Hatfield was returning northward from looking in on his horse down at the livery barn. Joe tied up in front of the jailhouse, waited, and, when Evan came along, Joe said: "Did you get a letter from Mister Hyland?"

Hatfield reacted with a grunt. He had tossed those three letters atop his desk before taking Enos Orcutt out back to wash and had not remembered them until right now. He led the way inside and, with Joe tugging off his gloves, picked up the envelopes, went slowly behind the desk as he opened them, and sat down when the last letter bore Hyland's signature.

Joe helped himself to a cup of coffee, and made a grimace after the first taste, but took the cup to a chair with him. Joe waited, and because Hatfield re-read Hyland's letter, Joe had plenty of time to finish his coffee before the sheriff spoke.

"He finished up at Albuquerque, and is now on his way up to Denver." Hatfield put the letter down and scowled at it. "He doesn't say a damned thing except that . . . he's finished at Albuquerque and is heading for Denver."

Lamont did not seem to be disappointed. "I got a letter from him, too, and he said he'd wrote to you."

"Anything in your letter?" the sheriff asked, and Joe answered almost indifferently.

"Not much. Some talk about the ranch, otherwise about what he told you." Lamont arose, plucking the gloves from under his shell belt. "Sheriff, I fired Art Daggett this morning."

That, then, accounted for the way Daggett had kept on riding south. Hatfield nodded but did not state that he thought the firing was a good idea. He did think so, though.

Lamont finished with his gloves. "I'm not plumb satisfied you and I look at this trespassin' business the same, but I know what you're trying to do. Mister Hyland would approve, so I guess I got to."

Hatfield arose, smiling. For a week now he had been fighting odds that had seemed to be multiplying right under his nose. This was the first encouragement he'd had, and, coming from Douglas Hyland's range boss, it was worthwhile. As he went around the desk, he said: "We got three separate views of this mess, Joe. Yours, mine, and the settlers' view. I'm square in the middle. But until Mister Hyland gets back, none of us is going to get off the hook."

Joe Lamont eased the door open slowly. "Maybe, when he gets home, Sheriff, it won't be any better. I can tell you one thing from working for him as long as I have . . . he don't give up."

They walked out front, stood a moment in overhang shade, then parted, and, as Joe Lamont rode away, Sheriff Hatfield walked up in the direction of the blacksmith's shop, a dingy, sooty building that was long and narrow and cluttered.

The red-faced man was there, with the blacksmith. Neither of them heard Evan Hatfield walk up. They were discussing a badly worn axle. The blacksmith was of the opinion than unless it were removed completely, built up at the forge, and re-tempered, it would not last three months, but the red-faced, gangling man thought a flux weld with the axle still under the wagon but while the wheel was off would get him by. The blacksmith looked around, saw the sheriff, and said: "Evan, we need a third opinion." It was amiably said. The blacksmith was a good-natured, easy-going man by nature, but when the red-faced man looked around, he spoke sharply.

"I don't need no cowman sheriff's

advice!"

The blacksmith's smile faded. He looked surprised, then he looked down at the worn axle and cleared his throat, plainly embarrassed.

The red-faced man said: "Just build it up right where it's standin' and I'll be on my way."

Finally, with his surprise gone and his next reaction taking its place, the blacksmith shook his head. "Mister, you better go somewhere else and get it fixed. Like I told you earlier, I don't have the time anyway."

The gangling man glared at the blacksmith. "You're like the rest, ain't you?"

Evan saw the smith's big fist tighten around the hammer he was holding. Before the smith could retort, Evan said: "Is your name Horne?"

The red-faced man swung around. "It is. And you're Hatfield. I heard about you last night."

Evan read the signs correctly. He had been facing things like this since the first week he'd pinned on his badge. In a quiet voice he said: "Mister Horne, I was going to ride out and visit with you this afternoon."

"You wouldn't be welcome at my camp, Sheriff."

Evan paused a moment. The blacksmith was staring at him. Hatfield and Horne understood all this, but the blacksmith, caught in the middle, was mystified. But whatever had brought this open hostility to the surface in his shop, he recognized the danger and resented it, so he said: "Mister Horne, I'm a busy man. I'll help you put this wheel on, then you can find someone else to build up the axle for you."

The settler was directly between them. They were both stalwart men, seasoned and oaken and one of them was armed. He turned, grasped the wheel in corded arms, and leaned to shove it over the axle. Not a word was said as he fitted the wheel, then twisted to snatch the nut from the blacksmith's outstretched hand.

Hatfield stood watching, and thinking. When the settler picked up the wrench to tighten the wheel nut, Hatfield said: "I aimed to come out to your camp and tell you what I've told the others . . . stay away from Arapaho Creek. By the end of next week we'll most likely have this settled, but until then stay off Hyland's range."

Horne gave the wheel nut a vicious

final twist, kept his back to Hatfield as he removed the wrench, then straightened around, clenching the big old wheel wrench, and glared. "I got title. All of us got deeds to that land. They're plumb legal and proper. I know what you're tryin' to do. We all know. You're owned by the cowmen. Hatfield, no one's goin' to keep us off land we filed on and got deeds to. No one."

Horne was waiting. Hatfield did not move. He had no fear of the man, or the wrench he was holding. "If you go out there," Evan said, "I'll lock you up for trespassing. Mister Horne, I don't personally give a damn who owns that land, but, until it's settled who does own it, I'm going to enforce the peace. That means, if you folks go out there, I'll be after you. . . . All you've got to do is wait a week. That's not a very long period of time, and after that, if it's proved you got the right, then I'll work the same way to protect your legal rights."

Horne seemed to be balancing between a decision to attack, or not to attack. Hatfield knew this, and the blacksmith also recognized it. The blacksmith stepped over and reached for the wheel wrench. Now, finally, he had made up his mind about what he had to do, but the moment his hand closed down around the wrench Horne swung. He was fast and agile. He was also tough as rawhide, and strong.

The blacksmith smothered the blow by being too close, but it staggered him. As he caught his balance, he growled, released his hold on the wrench, and sprang at the settler. Horne was taller by half a head, but the blacksmith was built like a barrel. When he catapulted into the settler, Horne tried to swing the wrench. The blacksmith was even closer now; there was no way for the settler to do more than glance the wrench off, and the blacksmith's fists were pumping like cast-iron pistons. He was enraged and bore in at the settler with unstoppable power.

Evan Hatfield, instead of breaking it up, stepped out of the way as the blacksmith jolted Horne against an anvil stand, then, with Horne's back against something unyielding, the blacksmith went after him. He made Horne's long arms turn loose and hang with a massive strike over the heart. He brought the taller man down in a knee-sprung sag with a fist to the side of the head, and, as Horne leaned, the blacksmith sledged him along the point of the jaw. Horne went down like a pole-axed steer, a trickle of scarlet at the corner of his mouth.

Hatfield finally moved between them, but the blacksmith was ready to stop. He looked down, breathed hard, looked up, and said: "He was mad at you, Sheriff, not me."

Hatfield was leaning to roll the unconscious settler flat out when he said: "He's mad at the world. He's mad at everyone who doesn't have to live out of a camp wagon. Give me a hand. We'll take him down the back alley to the jailhouse."

VIII

Enos Orcutt leaned on the front of his cage, watching as the blacksmith and the sheriff eased Horne down upon the straw-filled mattress of the wall bunk. When they left the cell room, Orcutt still leaned there, staring into the cell opposite him.

In the office the blacksmith declined Evan's offer of coffee, heaved a mighty sigh, and flexed sore knuckles. "Tell me one thing," he said to Hatfield. "What the hell was that all about?"

"Settlers filed on homestead land along Arapaho Creek. They got their deeds at the government Land Office up in Denver."

The blacksmith was quizzical. "But that's Hyland's range."

"Yeah. Mister Hyland's in Denver now, trying to straighten it out. Meanwhile, I'm trying to keep those people away from the creek."

The blacksmith looked at his sore hands. "They just come along to grab someone else's land without knowin' who it belonged to?" He wagged his head. "How many are there?"

"Three wagons of 'em so far, and the feller in the cell across from Horne. But there may be more on the way."

The blacksmith stared. "I never heard anythin' about this. I'll be damned." He went to the door and stepped out, then began wagging his head as he trudged back northward to his shop.

Hatfield returned to the cell room, but Horne was still as limp as a rag, so when Orcutt asked questions, Hatfield explained what had happened. Orcutt looked worriedly across the corridor. "He's been out a long time, Sheriff. Are you sure he isn't dead?"

Hatfield was sure. "He'll come around. He caught one hell of a punch on the jaw. When he sits up, I'd take it kindly if you'd try to talk sense into him. Just one more week, Mister Orcutt." Hatfield twisted to glance at the man on the wall bunk. "Maybe it'll be hopeless. I can tell you one thing about Mister Horne. He's got one hell of a temper." Hatfield faced forward again. "I'll go fetch you something to eat."

As he reëntered the office up front, the door was flung open from the plank walk outside, Otto Langer and Henry Schmidt stamped in, both of them wearing six-guns and shell belts, and there was no way to mis-read the expressions on their faces.

Hatfield was a believer in seizing the bull by the horns. Without wait-ing, he said: "If you're looking for your friend, he started a fight at the smithy, and now he's locked in one of my cells."

Schmidt glared, looking every bit as fierce and willing as Horne had looked an hour earlier. Otto Langer hooked thumbs in his gun belt and said: "We got a wagon outside. We'll take care of him back at camp."

Hatfield shook his head. "He stays, gents."

"On what charge, Sheriff?"

Hatfield stroked his jaw while reply-ing. "Disturbing the peace, provok-ing a fight." He dropped his hand.

"I'll think of something else."

Langer did not move. "He's entitled to bond."

Hatfield sighed. This was true enough. There was no justice court in Hyland. There was a circuit rider who appeared in town every couple of months, but short of murder, rustling, or horse theft, there were no common crimes that were considered serious enough for Hatfield to hold a prisoner that long. Moreover, he had a list showing a sliding scale of bail rates. Without consulting the list, Hatfield knew the fee for disturbing the peace — $3. For fighting it was the same, another $3.

But Hatfield had no intention of freeing Horne, so he said: "I can hold him twenty-four hours without a charge, gents."

Schmidt still glared, but he was silent. It was Langer, the taller man, who said: "We'll be back in twenty-four hours with the bail money. Right now, we're busy strikin' camp."

Hatfield knew better than to hope they were leaving Lost Valley. He studied the pair of them, had a bad premonition, and softly said: "What've you got in mind, gents?"

Now, finally, Henry Schmidt spoke. "We're goin' over onto our home-steaded land, Sheriff. We're going to set up camps and get to work. Summer don't last forever."

"Neither," responded Hatfield, "does my patience." He went closer to the desk and leaned there, big arms crossed over his chest. "One more week, gents. Make this easy on yourselves. I know you bought ammunition, and believe it or not I sympathize with you, but I've told you folks this until I'm getting tired of saying it . . . stay off Hyland's range until the matter of your deeds is cleared up. For your own sakes, stay away from there."

Schmidt turned fiercely toward the door, grabbed for the latch, and glared at Hatfield. "You're going to delay us as long as you can. One more week!" Schimdt sneered. "And next week it'll be the same . . . one more week. And after that. . . ."

He wrenched the door open and stormed out, leaving Otto Langer behind. Hatfield turned slowly. "I was hoping you'd have enough sense to be reasonable, Mister Langer. I was sort of hoping you'd be able to hold your friend back."

"I'm reasonable," the remaining settler said. "I'm even willing to sit doing nothing for another week. But like Henry said . . . after that week is up, there aren't any guarantees . . . are there, Sheriff?"

Hatfield side-stepped a direct answer. He had misgivings of his own, but he had no intention of sharing them with anyone, so he reverted to the main theme of their discussion by saying: "Don't cross the road, Mister Langer. Don't go over along the creek."

Langer remained motionless for a moment longer, then he also walked out of the office, but he did not say a word as he did so.

Hatfield leaned on the desk in thought for a while, then roused himself, went over to the café for beans and coffee for the prisoners, brought it back, and shoved two of the pails under Orcutt's door, then turned to face the venomous stare of the other emigrant. He leaned, shoved those two pails under, also, straightened up, and said: "You feel all right?"

Horne's response was savage. "You son-of-a-bitch. I'll get out of here one of these days, then you'll find out if I feel all right."

Hatfield considered the red-faced man. "The last man who called me that and meant it didn't wake up for two days. All right, Mister Horne, I'll be waiting when you get out."

He turned on his heel and went back up front, locked the cell-room door, and dropped the key atop his desk as he picked up his hat. He was not angry, but he was solidly convinced about what had to be done.

Over in front of the general store there were no loafers, which was unusual, it being still early with a warm sun shining. Up at the saloon he recruited two freighters, big bearded men in rough boots and checkered flannel shirts. He explained why he was rounding up a posse, but the freighters simply leaned on the bar, gripping beer mugs and grinning. They did not care in the slightest; all that mattered was that they would draw posse men's wages, four bits a day, ride livery horses they wouldn't have to pay for, and get an outing.

Over at the stage company's corral yard Evan had to explain to Frank Dimmer, the company's representative in Lost Valley, why he wanted to dragoon Frank's yardmen. All Frank said was: "Take 'em. I'll send all four of 'em down to your office. Just don't get 'em busted up because it's hard as hell to get good yardmen any more."

Hatfield trudged back to the jail-house, took down his booted Winchester, stuffed vest pockets with loads, and went behind the desk, stooped far down, dug out a bottle of malt whiskey, took two swallows, again hid the bottle, then went out front where the hostlers from the corral yard were coming up, armed with saddle guns as well as belt guns, and cocked an eye at the sun. There was plenty of time. It would take the settlers at least an hour to strike camp, unless they had already taken care of that before Langer and Schmidt walked over to town a while back.

The pair of freighters ambled through roadway dust on a diagonal course from the saloon. They still looked like men going on a coyote hunt, and, although both wore belted six-guns, Hatfield had to go back inside and bring out a pair of Winchesters. Then he led his posse down to the livery barn. Behind him, up and down both sides of the road, people came forth to watch, then to gang together in little excited groups.

The liveryman listened to Hatfield, then went with his day man to bring forth enough horses. He did not say a word until Hatfield's six armed men were leading their animals out front, leaving the sheriff and liveryman standing alone in the runway.

Then he spoke.

"It's them damned squatters, ain't it, Sheriff? I knew, even before I heard the talk around town last night, I knew them bastards would bring trouble with 'em. What folks ought to have done was ride out there some dark night, scatter their livestock, and burn their wagons."

Hatfield turned slowly. "You know a darned sight better'n to talk like that. There's not going to be any stampeding or burning. And if there is, I'll be after you first thing."

He led his horse out front, flintily looked at the grinning freighters, then swung up.

They rode northward up through town. People were ogling from the plank walk, and even more of them were doing the same from inside stores and from behind window curtains among the residences farther up toward the north end of town. Hatfield felt self-conscious, and just a little ludicrous, but there was no other way to get up along the north roadway, unless it was by riding several miles west, around town, then back again to the roadway, and that would take too long.

By Hatfield's calculations the settlers should be visible within the next hour or two. At the very most, two hours, and, because he felt confident they had struck their camp earlier, he thought now, as he led his riders up the stage road, the wagon tops would appear within an hour.

It was a long road and arrow-straight as far as the first rising swell of land eight or ten miles distant.

Beyond that it ran onward for another sixty or seventy miles before coming into any kind of broken country. The real mountains were twice that far, but they were distinctly visible and seemed much closer. It was another beautiful day, which should have had some influence upon how the sheriff felt, but he scarcely more than noticed it where he left the road, angling eastward. From this point on, his posse men became less talkative; it had been a pleasant ride among convivial companions up to this point. From here on, it might be different. Lawmen did not recruit posses for joy rides.

Finally Hatfield halted quite a way south of where he thought the wagons would cross, and, although there was no shade, the heat was not that objectionable. In fact, for a summer day, it was more like early autumn because there was a hint of briskness in the air.

One of the freighters piled off to lead his horse off a fair distance, then position the animal so that it was between the other posse men and his back. He stood wide-legged for a moment, then stamped his feet, and raised his head. The others were not interested; they were discussing with Evan Hatfield the possibility of having trouble with the emigrants. The man who had gone off to wet down the sagebrush turned to walk back as he called to Hatfield and gestured northward with an upflung arm.

"Wagon tracks yonder, Sheriff, and they're fresh."

The freighter was correct. Hatfield

sat his saddle up there, frowning at the ground. Langer and Schmidt already had their wagons moving when they came down to talk to him about releasing Horne. They had stolen a march on him.

One of the corral yard hostlers spat aside, stood in his stirrups, and quietly said: "By God, there's white tops a hell of a distance north and west, Sheriff, headin' toward Arapaho Creek."

Now Evan Hatfield was angry. He led off at a stiff trot. The canvas wagon tops were visible upon the west side of the road, and obviously Langer and Schmidt had made a fool of him. One of the bearded freighters said: "Sheriff, them folks didn't waste no time. They must have headed over before sunup. You can't drive big wagons that far otherwise. I know. I been doin' it all my growed-up life."

Hatfield did not take his eyes off the distant wagons, strung out one behind the other, three of them moving like laden ships in a light wind across a calm sea. He boosted his horse over into a lope. The men behind him did the same, and now there was no conversation at all. Trouble was something that left its aura along the back trail for many miles. Nor did posse men have to be experienced at this sort of thing to realize that this was not, after all, any joy ride.

Hatfield hauled back down to a walk when he was about a mile and a half distant. The wagons had halted down along the creek where willow shade partially camouflaged them.

They were not on the land Orcutt had a deed to, and they certainly were not far enough along to be on the land Langer and Schmidt claimed, which would be another mile or two westward, so what that halt signified was that the settlers had seen the horsemen coming, and had chosen the spot to make their stand.

Hatfield shook his head. He should have grabbed those two, Schmidt and Langer, when they were in his office. He should have jugged them both and flung the key out a window. He halted, raised a gloved large hand to halt the men behind, and sat on a low land swell gazing down where the settlers were occasionally visible, just the adults, which meant the children had either been told to remain inside the wagons, behind those musket-ball-proof oaken sideboards, or they had been hidden along the creek among the willows.

One of the bearded freighters made a shrewd study. "We can't hit 'em head on, and they got in among them willers, so's we can't sneak up ahind them. Who are they, Sheriff? There's one good head amongst them, I'd say."

Hatfield removed his gloves slowly, pocketed them without answering, and thumbed back his hat. The customary thing was to leave his guns behind and ride in down there with a hand in the air. A hell of a lot of good that would do. He'd already talked until he was blue in the face — and there they were, doing exactly what he had forbidden them to do. Talking was not going to do anything it had not accomplished before. He leaned and spat.

A corral yard hostler, dark with high cheek bones and black eyes, eased his horse around beside the sheriff. Hatfield knew the man; he was a Mexican who was reputed to have been one of the finest jerkline freighters in the business until a mule kick had broken his right elbow, leaving the arm partially stiff when it healed. Around town they called him Pancho, but his name actually was Guillermo. He jutted his chin as he said: "They got guns. I counted six by the sun flashes."

Hatfield looked around. "Six? There's only two men down there, Pancho."

The hostler grinned broadly. "They maybe got their woman armed, too.

Anyway, you set here and wait. When one of 'em moves, you watch the sun flashes."

Hatfield sat and watched because he had not yet decided what else to do, and the hostler was correct. He caught reflections of sunlight off six saddle gun barrels.

Then he remembered that someone had told him the man he had locked up back in town, Horne, had two half-grown sons. Langer, Schmidt, maybe their wives, and those two half-grown boys would account for six rifle barrels.

Someone muttered crossly. "Hell, it's even numbers, and I didn't bargain for nothing like that."

Hatfield hadn't bargained for anything like this, either, but then he hadn't bargained for the blasted wagons to be on the west side of the road, and there they were, with the horses off, the tongues in the grass, and not a soul showing except for an occasional reflection of sunlight off gun metal.

IX

No one liked being made to look foolish and Evan Hatfield was not an exception. Not only had they made him look foolish, but now they were in a fair way to turn him back with his tail tucked, and that would be even worse. There were four hostlers and two freighters who would tell the story of Sheriff Hatfield's rout when the posse got back to town. On the other hand, he was stubbornly adamant about a battle. Not simply because he objected on moral grounds, but also because in the back of his mind there was the lingering doubt about who did actually own that land, and, if a settler was killed by a posse and it turned out he was entirely justified in what he had been trying to do when they had shot him, Hatfield would have the U.S. marshal to face.

Time was passing. His posse men were fidgeting. One of them dismounted and squatted like an Indian in the shade of his drowsing horse.

Hatfield had to ride down there, but he had no illusions. Even if he had been a man of eloquent persuasion, which he certainly was not, the memory of Henry Schmidt's stubborn jaw and hostile eyes would have discouraged him. On the other hand, sitting out here in the sun doing nothing at all was even worse.

He said — "Let's go." — and lifted his rein hand.

Now, the posse men were totally silent. One of the freighters surreptitiously raised his booted Winchester a foot and slid back the slide to make certain there was a bullet under the hammer, something he should have done back in town.

The wagons were lined out about two tongue-lengths from one another. There was not a person in sight as the posse men walked their mounts down from the land swell toward the creek, but, by the time they were two-thirds of the way along, a man stepped around in front of the fore-most wagon, grounded a long-barreled rifle, and leaned on it, watching.

Someone said: "Damn, that ain't no carbine, that there is a rifle. He's got a quarter mile reach on us with that thing."

Hatfield answered curtly. "There's not going to be any shooting."

Again the posse men turned silent, but several of them exchanged looks. Maybe the sheriff did not want any shooting, but it always took two men with guns in their hands to make that binding, and the solitary tall man leaning on that rifle had a dampening effect.

It was Langer. Hatfield had thought it was before they were close enough to recognize one another. There were other rifle barrels scattered among the three wagons, clearly visible now without the aid of sunlight.

Hatfield said: "I'll go on alone. You fellers sit down and get comfortable."

There was plenty of grass to sit on, one of the hostlers observed as Hatfield walked his horse away, but there wasn't a worthwhile rock or a tree for protection, and grass didn't stop bullets.

Otto Langer straightened up, stepped across a wagon tongue, and went as far as the south side of his big old wagon. There, he leaned on the fore wheel, this time with his gun held crossways in both hands, and, when Hatfield was close enough, Langer said: "We're in the right, Sheriff."

Hatfield rested both hands atop the saddle horn as he gazed at the settler. "I told you . . . that's not the issue. It's going onto Hyland's range before this mess is settled. Hyland's not around, but his men are, and they've been chousing trespassers for a long while."

"We're not trespassers, Sheriff."

Hatfield swore under his breath. He was going to have to go around and around again, using the same argument against their same arguments. He tried something fresh. "Mister Langer, let me put this on a personal basis. My job is to enforce the law. It's also to preserve the peace, and that's more important to me than enforcing the damned law. I'd like to ask you folks to do me a personal favor . . . go back east of the road and wait over there for a few more days."

From the rear of the wagon, back where the tailgate chains were dangling, Henry Schmidt appeared, carrying one of those long-barreled rifles. He stamped forward and shook his gun at Hatfield. "We don't go back! When we move from here, we go forward, over where our land is." Schmidt stopped a yard or two from Hatfield's horse, his face red and his eyes hot with anger. "Personal favor? That's why you come out here with a posse of men with guns . . . to ask a personal favor? Hatfield, you're a hypocrite. You snuck up on William Horne, you tried to hold us back so's we'd freeze this winter, and now, because you see we're going to fight you, you're going to try and jolly us."

Evan braced into the wrath of the square-built man waving his rifle. He waited until Schmidt had ceased to speak, and waited another moment beyond that, then he said: "You're going back. One way or another, Mister Schmidt."

The burly man suddenly stopped gesticulating and stood stonestill as he swung the rifle to bear on Sheriff Hatfield. If he was going to speak, he lost the chance by not doing it immediately. Langer hauled up off the wheel and said: "Lower that gun, Henry."

Schmidt acted as though he had not heard. Hatfield did not believe Schmidt would shoot him, but he did believe that Schmidt could be driven to it by more arguing, so he sat, looking down and saying nothing.

Two gangling boys, both with the same red-sorrel hair Hatfield's latest prisoner had back in town, eased around from the farthest wagon, and a raw-boned graying woman as flat in front as a man ducked from inside the wagon. She, too, had a rifle in both hands.

Hatfield's cheek itched, but he made no move to raise either of his hands. Langer was staring at Henry Schmidt. "He'll leave, Otto. Lower the barrel."

Schmidt finally did lower it, but not all the way, and his regard of Evan Hatfield was exactly as it had been before: fierce.

Hatfield looked at them both. He had lost. Everything he could think of to say had been said before. He lifted his reins to turn away, and caught movement as a second woman moved into view from behind a wagon. He recognized her. She walked slowly up to the side of the first wagon, then stopped there. She had no weapon, and, as she and Sheriff Hatfield exchanged a look, he saw the fear in her face. He touched the brim of his hat to her and turned the horse.

Not a sound followed his departure among those people back there, nor did Evan glance around. Dead ahead his posse men were standing beside their horses. They had risen from the ground at the loud exclamations of Henry Schmidt, and had almost held their breath when Schmidt had aimed his gun at Hatfield.

From a considerable distance someone fired a handgun. It ordinarily meant simply that someone was beyond shouting range and wished to attract attention. Right now, a gunshot meant something else, and Hatfield reined back to a halt, his posse men spun in a new direction, and the people back down along the creek who had been moving closer to one another now spread out again, straining to see where the gunshot had come from.

Hatfield saw them long before the settlers did — six riders loping from the southwest all in a bunch. Hatfield rode on up to his posse men, swung to the ground, and stolidly identified the newcomers as Joe Lamont and the Lost Valley Ranch riding crew. Ordinarily at this time of the season they would not be riding over here — not the entire crew, anyway — but as Hatfield stood, watching their approach, he was not surprised. Nothing had gone right since breakfast time. Even so, he expected no trouble, although he anticipated Joe Lamont's annoyance and the truculence of his riders.

One of the hostlers said: "Now things're looking better. Now we got some support."

Lamont led his men at a lope to within a couple of hundred yards of the posse men, then hauled down to a steady walk, and, as they approached, they looked northward down along the creek where the wagons were. Evan Hatfield made a smoke, lit it, and waited. When Joe came on up, Evan nodded quietly, trickled smoke, and considered the faces of the riding crew. There was not a smile showing, not even an expression of resignation or philosophical acceptance of those people being down there along the creek.

Evan said: "They got over here before I could stop them, Joe."

Lamont surprised Hatfield by saying: "Did you try to stop them, Sheriff?"

Hatfield dropped the cigarette and ground it out. The last time he and Joe Lamont had discussed emigrants, Joe had said he understood Hatfield's position, but right now he was not acting like he understood it, or wanted to understand it. Hatfield raised his eyes and said: "What do you think I'm doing out here with a posse? I tried to stop them, yes, and a while back I went down and talked to them."

"Talked, Sheriff?"

"Told them to get back east of the stage road, Joe."

Lamont turned, glanced down toward the creek, and said: "I don't see anybody puttin' horses on the wagon tongues."

"We'll give them some time," said Hatfield, beginning to feel animus.

Joe turned back. "I don't know whether we will or not."

The range men, sitting clustered around their range boss, were listening, and watchful. Hatfield's posse men were the same. Those two freighters looked over Lamont and his riders without a trace of fear, but two of the corral yard man were beginning to fidget a little.

Hatfield returned Lamont's stare without difficulty. "We're all walking a tightrope, Joe. It's not going to help if we start fighting among ourselves."

Lamont's expression did not change, nor did he raise his voice, but there was no way to mistake how he felt about those trespassers along the creek. Even when the sheriff reminded him of their last meeting when Joe had sounded tolerant, at least understanding, the range boss' expression underwent no change, and he said: "Sure, I remember that, but we were talkin' about those people stayin' over east of the road, Sheriff. And I know what you're tryin' to do. I figure you're mostly right . . . but look down there. They're defying you and the law. They're defyin' Mister Hyland's rule against this sort of thing." Lamont eased up slightly in the saddle to lean on the horn. "Sheriff, mostly there's folks in this world don't understand anythin' but a big stick. But they sure as hell understand that. Those folks are goin' back east of the road, and they're goin' back today."

What lent particular substance to Lamont's pronouncement was the very quiet way he made it. Evan Hatfield, in a quandary again, had a moment to think some very uncharitable thoughts about Douglas Hyland, then he turned, snugged up his *cincha,* and swung up across leather, facing Lamont: "Joe, you chouse those people and we're going to lock horns." Then he gestured. "Ride off with me a little ways."

Hatfield had no intention of laying down the law to Lamont in front of his riders or the posse men. That would put Lamont into a position where he would have to save face by bucking the law.

As they walked their horses side-by-side away from the watching posse men and range riders, Lamont said: "Sheriff, they got to move. We can talk all day and nothing's going to change that. They can do their waitin' east of the road, but they're not goin' to do it down along the creek. You know what'll happen to me if they're camped down there when Mister Hyland gets back? He'll fire me."

"He won't do any such a thing, Joe. He knows as much about this mess as anyone . . . more than you and I know about it. He and I had a private talk before he left. He knows damned well what he left for you and me to sweat over. He won't fire you, not even if I've got to yank some slack out of him about that. Joe, leave this to me. I'll get them back east of the road, but you leave it to me. All they got to do is see a bunch of armed range riders circling their camp, and they'll dig in their heels."

Lamont stopped his horse, leaned on the saddle horn for a moment, then said: "I got the riding crew to think about, too. They know Mister Hyland don't tolerate anything like this. If I tolerate it, they're going to. . . ."

"Joe, damn it, I'm getting tired of sensitive feelings. You look them straight in the eye and say this is the law's business, and that's how it's going to be until Mister Hyland gets back." Hatfield turned his horse facing back the way they had come. "You can't run them off. Look down there. They're dug in and armed to the gills. If you make a fight of it, you're going to lose some men. Joe, you're also going to have the law against you, and the next time I ride out I'll bring half the damned countryside, and I'll haul the whole crew back and lock it up."

Lamont did not seem the slightest bit worried. In fact he sardonically smiled at Hatfield. "You couldn't raise ten men and you know it. Sheriff, I doubt like hell that you could raise two men to go against Lost Valley Ranch." Then, as Hatfield sat bitterly thinking that this was indeed true, and he had known it was when he'd been making his threat, Joe's sardonic smile lingered as he spoke again.

"But . . . all right, I'll take the crew home. We'll stay away from this part of the range until tomorrow afternoon. That ought to give you enough time to get those bastards out of here."

He and Hatfield exchanged a look, then the sheriff nodded, and they headed back where the other horsemen were waiting.

X

Hatfield was no better off after Lamont led his riding crew back in the direction of the home ranch than he had been before Lamont had arrived. In fact, he was in a worse situation, because now Lamont and his men knew the settlers were down along the creek. He had to take action. He'd made a promise to Lamont, and he'd issued a fiat to the emigrants. After watching the range men lope away, Hatfield left his posse men and rode back down to the wagons, and this time those two gangling sorrel-headed teenagers were alongside Langer and Schmidt and their women. That raw-boned, angular woman with the stringy iron-gray hair and the rifle was standing slightly apart from the others, bitterly watching Hatfield ride up. He assumed she was William Horne's wife, and the sorrel-headed big lads were his sons.

Henry Schmidt did not allow Hatfield time to speak. He said: "Now you're goin' to threaten us with those range men."

Evan drew rein, considered Henry Schmidt, for whom he was forming a thorough and deep dislike, and said: "I don't make threats, Mister Schmidt." He turned slightly to gaze at Otto Langer. "You folks've had time to talk it over . . . ?"

Langer nodded. "We talked. We're not going back."

"Four or five more days make that big a difference, Mister Langer?"

Schmidt interrupted. "No, Sheriff, four or five days don't make that much difference. But you're not goin' to let us come back over here in four or five days, and once we're back east of the coach road, you'll set up some kind of patrol to prevent us from gettin' back over here ever. And, Sheriff, we're here. If folks got to fight for their own, they're a sight better off being on their own land when they do it."

"This isn't the land you folks filed on. That'll be another few miles westerly."

Schmidt leaned on his rifle. "We know that. And by tomorrow morning we'll be on our own land . . . if we got to fight you every single yard of the way."

Hatfield gave up. He ranged a slow look at the women, those two frightened-faced but resolute lanky youths with their rifles, and turned back as he said: "You dug the hole, Mister Schmidt, I didn't."

He left them watching him ride back to the posse. He did not say a word, but gestured for the posse men to follow along as he walked his horse back in the direction of town. When they had passed over several lengthy low land swells and could no longer see the wagons, or the willow tops down along Arapaho Creek, one of the freighters could remain silent no longer, and said: "Sheriff, I expect maybe you did the right thing, but it's strange how folks look at something like this."

Evan faced half around. "You mean letting them run me off?"

"Yes."

"Well, mister, I'll tell you something I learned long ago. The man who makes a fast judgment is usually wrong as hell." The bearded man puzzled over that, and finally asked what it meant. Hatfield gestured toward the undulating country on both sides and said: "You go west and your partner go east. Leave your horses hobbled and scout up northward on foot. You know how to do that?"

The freighter knew. "You mean . . . scout up them settlers?"

"Yeah. Scout back and do it mostly on your belly, because, if they see either of you, it's going to pitch a monkey wrench into the works. You boys scout up there and watch that camp."

Hatfield drew rein. His posse men, mystified, also halted. They watched the sheriff study the sky before lowering his head to speak again. "We got maybe three hours of sunlight left." He paused to let that sink in. "Gents, after nightfall there won't be a moon for a couple hours. We're going back down without our spurs, skulk westward up the creek, cross it, and get behind the wagons."

The second freighter grinned broadly, but no one else did. "Hit 'em like Injuns," he opined, clearly delighted. "Jump 'em while they're outlined around their damned supper fire."

Hatfield gazed at the freighter. "Mister, we're not going to touch those people. We're going to take our guns, but we're not going to use them unless we absolutely have to."

"What, then?" demanded the freighter.

Hatfield answered curtly: "Horses, mister. We're going to steal their horses."

For a moment the men sat staring at Evan, then that Mexican-looking black-eyed hostler slapped his leg and laughed. The others finally reacted favorably, too, but not as enthusiastically as the Mexican-looking corral yard man, probably because they had never stolen horses, had grown up looking on horse stealing as ranking right up there with murder as the worst of all crimes, and finally because they had to be shocked that a sheriff who was charged with protecting property, including horses, would suggest such a thing.

Hatfield smiled a little. "They figure to drive farther across Hyland's land in the morning. Sure as hell that'll bring Hyland's riders back, and this time loaded for a battle. We're going to strand them right where they are. Then we'll palaver. If they want to move at all, they'll have to make a trade with me first. Otherwise, I'll impound their damned teams and it'll cost them cash money to redeem them."

One of the corral yard men stroked his stubbly jaw. "But, Mister Hatfield, Joe Lamont wants them plumb off his range. You're goin' to fix it so's they can't go back east of the road."

"I'll talk to Joe after we have their horses. Right now, I want to stop them from moving any deeper into Mister Hyland's range. We'll worry about getting them east of the road after we've set them afoot." He paused, regarding the posse men. "Anyone want to drop out and go home?"

If anyone wanted to, they did not have the nerve to say so. Hatfield led them westward for a mile, down in a swale, then swung off, and gestured for the freighters to break away. His last admonition to them was to repeat the warning he'd offered earlier.

"Don't let them see you. Hobble your horses a long way back in a gully or a swale. And stay out there until sundown. I want to be sure those folks don't hitch up and start moving tonight."

The freighters left in opposite directions, riding in a stiff trot. The other posse men swung down, loosened *cinchas*, hobbled their animals, and removed the bridles so each horse could crop grass unimpeded by the bit. The men sank down in the grass, fished for their tobacco or eyed the position of the sun, then got comfortable for a long wait as someone said — "Damn, goin' to miss supper tonight." — and someone else answered that tartly: "What d'you care? Old Barley ain't cooked a decent meal in his misbegotten life."

Evan Hatfield removed his saddle to have something to do, and swathed off his animal's back with twisted handfuls of buffalo grass — and thought. To impound livestock legally the animals had to be on someone's land where they had no right to be, and they had to be running loose. They were loose, across the creek in the willows, grazing, but whether they were on someone else's land brought up the original question that had caused all this trouble. Hatfield told himself his conscience would be clear because as far as he and everyone else in the territory knew, that was Douglas Hyland's range. Even if it wasn't, Hatfield had no proof of it now — this afternoon — and he could therefore in clear conscience embark on what he intended to do.

He finished with the horse, laid the saddle blanket hair side up to dry as much as possible before dusk, and strolled out a way along a thin roll of land, looking for his freighters. Neither of the men was in sight, and only one horse, small in the westerly distance, showed against the pale land with its creeping shadows. At that distance it could have been a ranch horse, a loose animal, except that horses did not ordinarily go off to graze by themselves if they knew where there were other horses on the range.

He strolled back with dusk on the way, had a smoke for supper, resaddled his animal, but left the *cincha* loose, then sank down where the posse men were speculatively looking at him. Hatfield said: "Well, short of having ourselves a war with those damned fools, I couldn't come up with any better way of neutralizing them."

A graying hostler commented dryly: "It'll neutralize 'em just fine, Sheriff. In this country a man can't go nowhere on foot. But they're going to come up screaming and clawing."

Hatfield smiled, leaned to stub out his smoke, and looked at the speaker. "It's a big country, *amigo.* They can claw and scream for ten miles in any direction." He yawned. "Sure wish I'd brought my saddlebags along. There's some mule jerky meat in them."

One of the freighters returned in a jog. He had been east of the dry camp, and, until his partner also returned, they would have to wait. All he had to report was that the emigrants were gathering firewood for their supper fire, and, excepting one sentry atop a high wagon seat with a rifle in the crook of his arm keeping watch, the emigrants seemed to be going about their normal routines.

The Mexican-looking man said: "Where are their horses?"

The freighter was loosening his *cincha* and answered without turning. "All I could make out was a pair of big grays west up the creek a hundred yards or so. But I'd guess the other horses was up in there, too, somewhere, only dark colors don't show up like them grays."

Shadows deepened and someone muttered about the other freighter. If they were going back down to the creek, which was a fair distance, the sooner they started the better.

The second freighter came back in

a casual walk as though he'd never been in a hurry in his life. "Nothin' much goin' on," he sang out as he dismounted and walked up to squat and lean on his carbine. "They're fixin' to eat supper . . . and right now I wish I was down there amongst 'em."

Hatfield arose, went out to pull loose his Winchester, then waited until the posse men were all making sure their horses would be here when they got back, then Hatfield sent the freighters back east and west again, each with a companion from the Hyland corral yard of the stage company. He elected to take that Mexican-looking hostler with him, and, before leading out, he admonished them again about being seen, or making any noise, or going close to the camp. They were to reach the creek on both ends of the wagon camp, cross it, and converge upon the far side with the other posse men, and they were to do it as prudently and warily as they could. They were not to hurry — what the hell, they had all night. He waited, and, when no one spoke, he gestured with his carbine.

The Mexican-looking hostler grinned as the other men faded away into the settling night. He said: "Sheriff, you ever sneak up and steal horses like this before?"

Hatfield looked down his nose. "No."

The hostler was not abashed to admit that he had. "When I was a buckaroo down along the Sonora border, I used to steal horses. Down there, it's how you make a living. Otherwise you starve."

Hatfield was not particularly interested so he said: "Come along."

It was a long hike. Hatfield had never cared much for long walks. Being a large, heavy-boned, muscular man he did not consider himself built for walking. One of the obvious natural laws of God, or someone anyway, was simply that horses had four legs and big stout bodies, along with very small brains, while men had only two spindly legs and much larger brains. It naturally followed, then, that men should ride horses. Hatfield had been riding horses, and avoiding this sort of walking all his life.

The hostler, though, was a wiry man who could keep up with Hatfield's longer stride and talk at the same time. He seemed to be enjoying himself.

It was farther than Hatfield thought. Or maybe it wasn't really any farther; it just seemed that way when a man had to cover all that undulating prairie land on foot, but by the time he was northward into the area where cooler air from the creek was noticeable, Hatfield felt that he'd probably covered more miles without halting to rest than he'd ever done before on foot.

The Mexican became quieter, more Indian-like in his attitude. He stepped close and spoke in a lowered voice as he gestured westward. "Got to go up there, Sheriff. I didn't see no dogs with them people, but a little breeze is blowing away from the camp westerly."

Hatfield leaned on his carbine, gazing down where a faint flicker of supper fire showed occasional sparks and a middling flame against the dark world along the creek. He sighed and straightened up to lift the carbine and move forward again. "You know," he said solemnly, "my daddy was a harness maker. He wanted me to follow the trade, too. He said there'd never be a day when a harness maker wouldn't be in big demand. . . ."

The hostler's white teeth flashed in the darkness. "But no, and here you are walking on foot like a peon, in the darkness, to steal someone's horses."

Hatfield saw the grin and smiled back.

They angled northward with the scent of creek greenery in their faces.

Now and then a vagrant scent of wood smoke came up to them, also, but not very often until they were angling down the last slope before reaching the creek. There the smoke fragrance was steadier, which meant the hostler had been right back there, the little evening breeze did in fact flow from east to west.

Once Hatfield picked up a snatch of words, indistinguishable but un-mistakable, and altered course so that they would reach the creek farther westward. They had to move more slowly, once they got into the spongy footing along the creek, because the grass was thicker than the hair on a dog's back and ten times as matted and wiry. One misstep would send a man sprawling into creek-side mud.

Hatfield paused to listen while the

Mexican went forward. The night out here was as silent as the inside of a grave, and, while Hatfield had worried all the way down here that his posse men would make noise, now he was worried that they hadn't made any. The hostler returned from weaving back and forth through willows and thorny berry bushes to whisper that he had found a way to cross over. He also said — "I smell horses." — and pointed eastward.

Hatfield smelled nothing but rotting vegetation and mud. He followed his guide, got raked several times with berry tendrils that possessed dagger-like thick thorns, and smothered the natural profanity that arose to his lips each time it happened.

Then he stepped through a rind of mud into water and felt his way.

Ahead, the hostler was moving like a leather-colored wraith. Arapaho Creek was not deep this time of year, although during winter snow run-off or spring deluges it spread a mile outside both its banks and drowned livestock every year.

They reached the far side, a matter of perhaps four or five yards, kicked off surplus mud and water, went ahead to the matted grass, and leaned to skive off the mud that had not been scuffed off.

Hatfield arose to look left and right, then walked farther northward to get clear of the willows and be in open country again. His companion brushed the sheriff's sleeve and made a gesture with two fingers. Hatfield nodded, and the Mexican turned southward, hanging close to the willows for camouflage and was lost to sight in moments.

Hatfield grinned to himself where he halted to lean on the saddle gun. The next time he had to do something like this he'd make a particular point of taking that Mexican with him.

XI

The Mexican found their posse men friends a considerable distance southward, and brought them back by going far out and around until, when they approached Hatfield, they were coming almost directly southward. He lay in the grass with his saddle gun shoved ahead until he was positive, then arose to ease down the hammer.

The other posse men, though, did not appear until Hatfield was beginning to mutter profanely, and even then the posse men skulked in one at a time as though they were scalp-hunting strong hearts making a stalk.

The Mexican knew where the horses were. He had encountered them on his southward search. He also knew something else. "There's a man in among the willows with them. He's got one of those long-barreled rifles."

Hatfield said: "Just one man?"

The Mexican elaborately shrugged, turned without a word, and faded out in gloom and tree shadows.

A thoughtless corral yard man leaned aside his gun to roll a smoke. One of the freighters did not open his mouth; he leaned and struck the troughed paper, sending flakes of tobacco to the grass. The corral yard man jerked indignantly upright, but all his companions were gazing stonily at him, so he turned away in mild embarrassment.

The Mexican returned. "They got the horses tied. Haltered and tied. They're standin' in there full as ticks."

Hatfield was more concerned with the sentry. "Only one man watching them?"

"Only one, and he's sitting down with his back to a willow. Maybe he's asleep."

Hatfield gestured. "Lead the way. Quiet now. Damned quiet."

They had close to a mile to travel before the Mexican raised a hand, then disappeared again, but this time he reappeared almost instantly, grinning. No one else was smiling. With both palms pressed together he put his hands to his cheek and leaned his head in the position of a sleeping person. Then he grinned again and pointed. Hatfield considered. Clearly they had to be sure of the sentry first, then get the horses. He motioned for the Mexican to head back, and now as each posse man walked through the spongy grass and creek willows, they particularly watched each step.

It wasn't a man sitting there asleep propped against a big willow; it was one of those gangling sorrel-headed youths, which disappointed Sheriff Hatfield. He had hoped the sentry might be Henry Schmidt. He would have no qualms about hitting

Schmidt over the head with a gun barrel.

They got up to within twenty feet of the slumbering sentry, and halted, as motionless and silent as wraiths. The Mexican was grinning again. Evan Hatfield stepped closer, eased down to one knee, studied the raw-boned youngster, then slowly raised one hand to the slumbering sentry's face and the other one to his gullet. Then he moved, bearing the youth over backward and to one side into the spongy grass where Hatfield could smother the sudden wildly flailing of arms and legs until his companions could each grab an extremity and spread-eagle the youth, whose eyes were starting from his head.

Hatfield kept one hand over the

youth's mouth and the fingers of the other hand closing around the youth's windpipe. He allowed air to pass into the boy's lungs but did not ease up his silencing grip until the youth stopped fighting. Then Hatfield said: "Son, not a sound out of you. Not so much as a sigh. You understand? Because we could have split your head open to keep you quiet, and we didn't, so now just sit up and be quiet. All right?"

For five seconds the boy was rigid, then gradually, as his body loosened, Hatfield removed the hand from his gullet, grabbed shirt cloth, and pulled the boy up into a sitting position. Then he said: "Not a sound. Agreed?"

The lad unsteadily nodded his head.

Hatfield removed the remaining hand, heard the boy gulp air, and waited briefly. Then Hatfield rocked back on his heels. "Son, you got a choice. Go with us or stay here. If you want to stay here with your folks, we've got to tie you and gag you. If you go with us, you'll be taken to the jailhouse in town. Which'll it be?"

Perhaps Hatfield's calm words without menace in them helped the sorrel-headed youth recover, but in any event he said: "I don't want to go with you, Sheriff."

Hatfield was agreeable. "Give me your belt," he said, and leaned to wrap the boy's ankles with the belt and lash them tightly. Then he said: "Are any of these horses broken to ride?"

The boy, looking up at the closed-down faces of the posse men, two of whom were fully bearded and villainous-appearing in the darkness, swallowed with effort, then pointed. "That there bay horse, and the seal-brown ahind him, and that old gutsy gray mare. The other horses is only broke to pull."

The Mexican leaned to offer Hatfield a length of braided rope he used to keep his trousers up. Hatfield tied the lad's hands behind his back, eased him down in the grass, and felt for the youth's blue bandanna to use as a gag.

The Mexican used his own bandanna through two front loops to improvise a method to prevent disaster when he moved.

The boy's round eyes followed their moves as each man went toward a tethered horse. Hatfield chose the gutsy old gray mare, which turned out to be mean; she tried to bite his hand when he reached to untie her. Any other time Hatfield would have slapped her, but right now he did not want a horse fight on his hands, so all he did was call her a fierce name in a whisper.

It went off more smoothly than Hatfield had expected it to. They led the horses northward out beyond the willows, and kept leading them westward for a half mile before one of the hostlers turned the bay he was leading, wrapped a war bridle around its nose, made of the lead shank, and vaulted onto the horse's back. Nothing happened. The bay horse dutifully plodded along.

Twice Hatfield tried to mount the

old brood mare, and both times as he turned to spring up, she bit his rear pockets. The third time he shortened the far side length of rope and made it up. The posse men leading team horses had to walk, but no one resented that now. All they wanted to do was get back across the creek and beyond rifle range of the wagon camp.

They probably would have made it except that one of the thousand-pound light harness horses balked at wading out into what must have looked to him like a black morass of deadly quicksand. The hostlers swore and larruped him. He still balked. Hatfield and the Mexican rode their saddle animals up and leaned their combined weight forcing the team horse to yield, but he did it by sucking back and giving a tremendous leap, attempting to reach solid footing upon the far side. The man holding his shank was jerked a foot into the air, then was dragged belly down through mud and water and more mud, but to his credit he did not relinquish his grip. Then the trembling horse tried to kick free of the rope, and in this fit of anger he whinnied the shrill, high call of a horse in distress.

One of the hostlers rode up close, aimed a big balled up fist, and struck the horse squarely between the eyes. Only a very angry or reckless man would do anything like that, but it made the horse momentarily wilt and bat his eyes, and by then his mud-covered handler was able to stand up and renew his grip.

Hatfield motioned for them to move along. That soggy, muddy hostler accepted the offer of the bay horse from the Mexican, led his recalcitrant harness horse in close, and broke clear upon the south side of Arapaho Creek at about the same time the moon appeared.

They were about a mile and a half west of the wagon camp when they left the creek riding southward — and heard a man's swift, high call of alarm back down along the creek somewhere.

One of the freighters abruptly changed course, heading more to the west. It was safe to assume he was thinking of the range of those rifles back yonder. But they got two miles southward with undulating land swells between them and the creek without another incident. Where they finally halted, they were beyond the sight of anyone back down along the creek.

That dragged man got down, pulled grass, and proceeded to rid himself of as much of the foul-smelling mud as he could. When he looked up and saw Sheriff Hatfield watching, the man said: "Somebody . . . you or them settlers back yonder, or the Hyland town council . . . owes me a new pair of britches and a new shirt."

Another posse man held up a hand. "I think I busted some knuckles on that damned horse back at the creek."

One of the bearded freighters shook his head. "Anybody'd know better'n punch a horse in the forehead, friend. If you want to get their attention like that, hit 'em on the nose where there ain't no bone."

Hatfield leaned to listen. He let the talk around him continue for a few moments before he growled for silence and got it. Then they all listened.

Not a sound came out to them although Hatfield had no doubt but that by now the settlers had found the terrified boy, and also had found that their horses were gone. He sighed and said: "Let's get our own horses and head for town, gents."

No one had much of an idea about the time, but, judging from the position of the moon as they plodded along, once astride their own saddles and leading the settlers' horses, Hatfield thought it had to be around midnight.

He was correct. By the time they

had Hyland in sight the only lights visible were from two guttering old carriage lamps down at the lower end of town, one on each side of the broad doorless opening of the livery barn, and another brighter light in the front window of the general store. Otherwise, Hyland was not only dark, it was utterly hushed.

They corralled the horses in one of the public pens out behind the livery barn, routed out a night man to care for their own horses, and at his big-eyed stare the posse men turned their backs to walk up front to the road-way, following the sheriff.

Hatfield crossed on an angle in the direction of the totally dark café. He banged on the door until the entire wall shook, waited, then pounded again. A lamp flickered to life somewhere out back. Hatfield rattled the wall a third time, and now he got a reaction — an irate string of blistering profanity as old Barley Smith came charging forward with his lamp held high in his left hand and his old Colt .44 in the other hand, purple in the face. He flung back the door and jumped, wide-legged, into the opening, waving the six-gun. The man who was covered with creek-mud struck the gun aside, stepped in, and shoved his face within inches of Barley's nose, snarling furiously. They all bumped past Barley, bouncing him back and forth. Hatfield lit the counter lamp, set it down, hard, and turned.

"Just bring it out here. Whatever it is, just fetch it out here with some spoons to eat it with."

Barley let the Colt dangle at his side. His nightdress hung, slack and voluminous in the poor light, as he stared and wrinkled his nose. "You fellers smell like a tan yard, for Christ's sake. And I don't feed folks after nine o'clock, and by God every one of you know that!"

Hatfield looked steadily at his old friend. "Barley, we just stole a herd of horses, and we've been all day without a blessed mouthful to eat. Now you fetch it out. Never mind if it's in a stew pot, just bring it out here."

Barley stared from Hatfield to the other soiled, rumpled, muddy, tired, and beard-stubbled men. "You stole someone's horses? Evan, what in the hell . . . ?"

"Barley, if you don't bring out that

food, we're going to go back there and get it ourselves."

Smith shuffled around the far corner of his counter, put down his own lamp while moving toward the old blanket that cordoned off his cooking area, and, as he passed Hatfield, he rolled his eyes. "Stole horses . . . ? Evan, I can't feed anybody cold stew. It'll give you the grip. Set down and I'll warm it up. I'll fetch some coffee. You been out tonight stealing horses, Evan Hatfield?"

They eased down along the counter. When the coffee came, they slid the pot back and forth until it was empty. By then there was the aroma of cooking food coming from behind the old blanket.

Hatfield looked at the mud-stained corral yard man and wagged his head. The corral yard man shook his head, too, then he laughed, and they all laughed at the grotesque sight he made.

XII

Hatfield fed his prisoners a late breakfast because he had not awakened until long after the sun had risen, and, while he was in the cell room, he had to listen to their loud and indignant imprecations because he had not fed them the day before. To silence them he said: "Got sort of busy yesterday and last night, trying to keep your friends from getting hurt. They moved your settler camp down along the creek. Hyland's riders found them down there. If I hadn't been down there, too, with a posse, there would have been some fur flying. Then, last night, I took all their horses and brought them here to town."

Horne and Enos Orcutt stared out of their cells, for the time being unmindful of the food at their feet regardless of their hunger.

Hatfield returned to the office to fire up the wood stove under his coffee pot. He had hardly got seated at the desk when Joe Lamont walked in, tugging off his gloves and soberly nodding at the seated lawman. Lamont kicked a chair around, dropped into it, and crookedly smiled. "I saw the horses down at the public corral, Sheriff. I left a man down there to keep an eye on them. We went down along the creek early this morning."

Lamont's crooked smile widened a little. "You got some awful mad settlers down there. They had the gall to ask us to loan 'em some horses."

The office, which normally smelled of stale tobacco smoke, was beginning now to smell of heating coffee. It was a pleasant fragrance.

Hatfield leaned back. "They were going on westward to hunt up the land they got title to. I had an idea you might not take kindly to that."

"So you stranded them. All right, Sheriff . . . but that don't get them off our range, does it?"

"Joe, when I was a young man, I was in the war down South. An awful lot of men were struggling like hell to accomplish things that seemed to me never to get accomplished. Only part of them did. I came out of that war convinced of one thing . . . the best a man can do, if he's got other men doggedly set against him, is part of what he's trying to do. Last night I had to settle for keeping those emigrants grounded in place. It's a compromise, but at least it's holding them plumb still." Hatfield sniffed the coffee. "Care for some java?"

Joe was agreeable, and he smiled at Hatfield's broad back, not because he particularly sympathized with what Hatfield was trying to do, although deep down he did sympathize with it, but because he could still remember the foot-stamping wrath and exasperation of those stranded emigrants. He and his riders had laughed about that all the way to town.

When Hatfield returned with two

cups, Joe accepted one of them with a dry remark. "They're madder'n wet hens."

Hatfield went to his chair willing to believe that. "Being mad's better'n being dead, Joe."

Lamont finally laughed aloud and Hatfield, sipping coffee, showed a twinkle in his eyes over the rim of the coffee cup. "Pretty mad, eh?"

Lamont lowered his cup. "Mad? I never saw folks so mad. There's a short, bull-necked feller, must weigh close to a hundred and ninety-five pounds, got arms on him like oak logs. He would have fought us two at a time if we'd've climbed down."

Hatfield said: "Schmidt."

"And there's a raw-boned gray-headed woman. She's got a temper like a tarantula. She blessed us up one side and down the other, until that feller called Langer stepped in."

"They thought you stole their horses?"

"Yeah. Sheriff, if I'd known anything about that, I wouldn't have rode down there. Those folks was mad enough to shoot someone. This Langer feller had a gawky big kid with him. The kid said it wasn't none of us, and after that things sort of settled down." Lamont drained his cup. "You're goin' to have trouble to your gills when they get to town and find their horses here. They don't much care for you anyway."

Hatfield could be philosophical about that; he did not much care for those emigrants. "It's a long walk, Joe."

Lamont did not dispute that. "Sure

is. But they'll make it. People like that can walk all day, like an Indian, so they'll make it." Lamont arose and put his empty cup aside. "Sheriff, you better lock 'em up. That one bull-built feller is nothing but trouble four ways from the middle. The other feller's not as bad, maybe, but he was mad as hell, too."

Hatfield went to the boardwalk out front with Lamont. "I got two in the cells now, and I only have three cells."

Lamont turned and led his horse over to the tie rack in front of the general store, where several of his men were loafing, apparently waiting.

Hatfield was turning back into his office when two men rode up and swung down, and one softly said: "Sheriff . . . ?"

Hatfield turned. From their droopy hats to their flat-heeled heavy cowhide boots they were emigrants, although both rode good outfits and both carried six-gun leather shaped to the bodies of each wearer.

Hatfield nodded and held the door for the strangers to enter his office first, then he hospitably offered them coffee. Both declined. One of them was a broad-faced, slate-eyed individual with gray around the temples and a pleasant expression. The other stranger seemed more inward, more reticent and wary.

It was the pleasant-faced one who said: "I'm Cal Arbuckle. This here is Harry Dent. We just reached Hyland this morning." Arbuckle leaned to fish inside his coat. When he brought forth a folded, rough-textured map,

Hatfield went wordlessly to his desk and sank down.

"You filed on some land," he said flatly. "Mister Arbuckle, I've seen those maps before."

The pleasant-faced man looked inquiringly at the sheriff. "You don't like the notion of settlers, Sheriff?"

Hatfield side-stepped a direct answer. "Is your claim along a creek, Mister Arbuckle?"

"Yes, sir. Along an unnamed creek."

"It's got a name. It's known as Arapaho Creek. If those land people in Denver know enough to draw maps, I wonder why in hell they don't know enough to give the creek its proper name."

The second man shifted slightly in his chair. "Those are old maps," he said quietly. "By trade I'm a surveyor.

I served eight years with the Topographical Corps of the Army. I been hiring out to make surveys ever since. They have old maps in the Land Office, but they're good. Just too old, I guess, to have proper names on them."

Hatfield eyed this quiet man more closely. "You're a surveyor by trade, Mister Dent?"

"Yes, sir. And a homesteader right now, by choice."

"Did they tell you fellers over in Denver that the title to the land along that unnamed creek was in dispute?"

Both the men stared. Evidently nothing like this had been mentioned in Denver, or anywhere else these two men had been. Arbuckle finally said: "Dispute with cattlemen, Sheriff?"

"With one cowman, Mister Arbuckle. With Douglas Hyland whose grandfather got title to it from the Mexicans before you or I were born."

Harry Dent looked slightly dolorous. "Sheriff, those old Mexican deeds about half the time were not worth the paper they were written on. After the Mexican War our government set up a commission to verify or deny the legality of Mexican grants. They verified very few, but they denied hundreds of them."

Hatfield was facing a different variety of settler this time. Neither of these weathered, seasoned men got angry, raised his voice, or showed solid intransigence. But Hatfield was not ready to let down his guard. If anything, he was particularly leery of these two. Men like Langer and Schmidt were predictable; these two were not.

"The problem right now is, gents, I don't want trouble on the range, so I'm forbidding settlers to go west of the stage road for another few days, until Mister Hyland gets back with the exact standing of his Mexican deeds. . . . I've got two settlers locked in my cells, and yesterday I stopped three wagonloads more from going any farther across Mister Hyland's range. You two . . . make it easy for me and for yourselves for a few days . . . either stay in town, or make a camp, whichever you have in mind, but don't ride west of the roadway."

Surprisingly both the armed settlers nodded their heads. Hatfield eyed them with suspicion. As they arose, Cal Arbuckle said: "We don't want trouble, Sheriff. How long before

Mister Hyland gets back to town?"

"Couple of days, more than likely. He's been gone two weeks and that's all he expected to be gone."

Arbuckle accepted this. "Fine. We'll make a camp over east of town."

Hatfield stood in his office doorway, watching Arbuckle and Dent ride slowly back up through town, trying to decide whether he trusted them or not. From behind him on the plank walk someone said: "Sheriff!" When he leaned and turned, the fist was a blur. He had one second to react, which was not quite enough time, but instinctively he lowered his head and the rock-hard set of knuckles bounced off his skull, knocked his hat off, and made him see stars for a second, then he was moving away from the door, moving backward, yielding ground as the blurry distorted features of Henry Schmidt swam toward him through the momentary mist of being stunned.

Across the road where Joe Lamont and his riders were getting ready to mount up out in front of the general store, someone yelped in astonishment. Hatfield heard that, but it scarcely registered as he continued to give ground before the enraged settler.

Schmidt was after Hatfield like a badger. He came in swinging powerful arms, his body thrusting forward, his teeth bared in a soundless snarl. For the sheriff there was no time to overcome his astonishment; there was only time to try and avoid those granite fists and the onrush of the furious emigrant. Twice Schmidt scored, and each time Hatfield sagged. It was like being kicked by a mule. Schmidt had equal force in either hand, and clearly he was experienced at this sort of thing.

Evan Hatfield continued to give ground until his head was clear, then he pawed outward to spoil Schmidt's aim, stepped off the duckboards into roadway dust, and, when Schmidt launched himself forward, also stepping off the sidewalk, Hatfield caught the settler with one foot in the air. Hatfield, too, could hit hard. Schmidt grunted, temporarily lost his footing, moved sideways until he had regained it, and hauled up a curving shoulder to protect his face, and started in again.

Hatfield feinted, but Schmidt did not come ahead. Hatfield baited the shorter, thicker man, then side-stepped — and Schmidt was there to swing a punch that grazed Hatfield's shoulder. It dawned on the sheriff gradually that he was not fighting just an enraged settler, he was up against a man who knew more about this kind of fighting than Hatfield knew.

He kept away, pawed at Schmidt to keep him off, and tried circling to the left. Schmidt did not lift his feet to turn; he shuffled around in the dust, never being unprepared. Hatfield tried circling in the opposite direction. The same thing happened again. Hatfield stepped two paces to the right, one back to the left, and fired a fist straight through Schmidt's guard, and that time the heavier man wilted. Hatfield went in fast, swinging hard and trying to get the full weight of his entire body behind each blow. He was fighting desperately now.

Schmidt weathered most of the blows, massive arms up to protect his face and jaw, but Hatfield aimed lower, hit Schmidt over the heart with his body twisting in behind the strike, and that time Schmidt's arms dropped, his face contorted, and his eyes mirrored pain.

Until this moment Hatfield had heard nothing and had seen only Henry Schmidt, but when he stepped back to gulp air and lower his arms for a moment of respite, the cries of Lamont's riders and a dozen or so townsmen, along with their motions and contorted faces coming into focus, showed Hatfield that he and Schmidt were in the center of a ring of excited spectators. Evan raised his arms with an effort, and went in again. Henry Schmidt was slow to react, but he got his guard up, only this time it was lower to protect his body, and Hatfield aimed higher.

Hitting Schmidt along the jaw was like hitting a stone wall. Most other men would have collapsed. Schmidt bobbed and weaved, took the blows and tried to protect his chin within the bend of a hunched-forward shoulder, but now he was on the defensive. Hatfield was still not angry, but his arms felt as though each one weighed a ton, and his lungs were afire as he continued to push forward. Finally Henry Schmidt gave ground for the first time, and the spectators yelled and roared, gesticulating with their fists and stirring dust as they moved around to see better.

The sheriff battered away, never missing, but no longer with the power he'd had earlier. Then he suddenly stepped back and dropped both arms. There was blood at the corner of Schmidt's mouth, and his right eye was puffily closing.

Hatfield sucked air a moment, gazing at his adversary, then he said: "Go on into the jailhouse, Mister Schmidt."

Without a word or another gesture, Henry Schmidt turned none too steadily, and, where the crowd parted to let him through, men hooted their derision that he ignored. He groped for the door latch. A spectator leaned, opened the door, and stepped back.

Men thumped Hatfield's back as he, too, walked across to the door and went inside. They probably would have also crowded in, but Hatfield kicked the door closed at his back.

Schmidt sank down upon a bench, hung his face in both hands, and faintly blood trickled to the floor. His breathing was as loud as that of a wind-broke horse.

Hatfield went behind the desk, leaned far down to rummage, and brought up his hidden whiskey bottle. He filled two glasses, topped off the upper half with water, and went over to push a glass at the settler.

"Take it," he commanded. Schmidt complied, straightening up as though his ribs and stomach pained him.

Hatfield went over to the edge of the desk, leaned, gulped air, shook off sweat, and gazed at the heavier man. "Drink it," he said. Again

Schmidt complied.

Hatfield sipped his branch water and whiskey, remained silent until his breathing got closer to normal, then he went to the desk chair and eased down. He knew how Schmidt felt because he did not feel any better.

The whiskey helped. Hatfield put the glass aside and examined his skinned, battered hands. Schmidt was sitting up now, drinking as though the glass held medicine. His eye was almost closed. It was also turning slightly blue above and below. There were other contusions, but the broken lip at the corner of his mouth was swelling and it lent him the appearance of a man ready to sob.

Hatfield finally said: "Where's Langer?"

Schmidt's answer was prompt, but

his injured mouth made the words thick. "Back at camp. I came alone. Langer didn't know I was coming."

Hatfield looked up. "Alone? You came in here looking for a fight, alone?" He wagged his head. "You're not very smart, Mister Schmidt. If you'd put me down, they'd have probably strung you up."

"You stole our horses!"

"Sure did. They're down at the public corrals, impounded by the law."

"You're the one that broke the law!"

Hatfield finished his whiskey and water and eased back in his chair. He steadily gazed at the battered, square-jawed settler, then he said — "Hell." — in a tone of monumental disgust and arose. "Empty your pockets on the desk, and hoist your britches legs so's I can see if you've got any hide-out weapons."

Schmidt was slow to arise, but Hatfield was in no hurry. Maybe Joe Lamont had been correct; maybe he was going to have to lock up every blasted one of them.

XIII

It was said that trouble, like rattlesnakes, came in pairs. Evan Hatfield was out back at the wash rack in the alley, using cold water on his bruised face and hands when Steve Clampitt came into the empty office and sang out. Hatfield stepped to the open back door and growled, then stepped back to his basin of cold water.

Clampitt had his storekeeper's

apron rolled up and tucked into his belt. He looked in awe at Evan's bruises, but tactfully did not mention the fight, which he had seen through a window across the road. Instead he said: "There was a feller looking for you over at the store, Evan."

Hatfield reached for the towel. "What feller? Is he blind? The jailhouse has a sign over it."

Clampitt digested this surliness with a flinch. "Federal lawman, Evan."

Hatfield lowered the towel and turned. "Did he say that's what he was?"

"Well, no, but when he fished in a pocket to pay for the stogies he bought, I saw the little badge on his vest under the coat."

Hatfield leaned to peer in the wavery mirror at his face. "You want to know something, Steve? That little sawed-off son-of-a-bitch can hit like a stud horse."

Clampitt, about to comment on Hatfield's bruised face, changed his mind at the last moment and said: "I guess that deputy federal lawman was over here, looked in, and you was out back. Anyway, he asked about you . . . where you might be and all."

Hatfield reset his hat, flung away the water, hung the basin from its nail, and turned with the towel in his hand. "Thanks. I'll look him up. Care for some coffee?"

Clampitt declined the coffee but trooped inside behind the sheriff, then went out the roadway door back across to his store, having done his good deed for the day.

Hatfield went over to the café, had Barley fix three pails of stew and coffee, and, at the inquiring look he got, Hatfield said: "For the battling settler. Now I got every cell full."

Barley was not and never had been a tactful man. Unlike Steve Clampitt, Barley cocked his head, squinted, then said: "He got you a few times. Want to know what I think?"

Hatfield sat down at the counter. "Sure."

"That feller's fought for money, somewhere."

Hatfield had arrived at this same conclusion during the battle. "Fill me a cup of stew first, and I'll be eating it while you're making up the pails."

Barley nodded, making no move to depart. "But you gave one hell of an accountin' for yourself. Fellers around town are saying you're just as good now as you was ten years ago."

Hatfield sighed. "The stew, Barley." There was no one in the town of Hyland who knew how good Evan Hatfield had been ten years ago.

He was eating his bowl of antelope stew when the stranger walked in, nodded amiably, sat down. When Barley poked his face around the blanket partition, the, stranger said — "A bowl of the same." — then he watched Hatfield for a moment, considered the purple splotches and swellings, and said: "You're a hard man to get hold of, Sheriff."

Hatfield did not look up. He knew who the stranger was. "Not if you holler when you poke your head in the office doorway."

The stranger smiled. "I'll remember

that." He extended a big hand, palm up, holding the circlet-and-star badge, so Hatfield could see it. "Deputy U.S. marshal from Denver." He closed his hand and pocketed the little badge. "Name's Charley Wheaton."

Hatfield finished the stew and shoved away the bowl as he straightened back for a look at the federal officer. Wheaton looked average in just about every way, except in the dead-level, stone-steady way he returned Evan's look. He was perhaps forty years old, tanned, lean, and loose-looking. Hatfield, who was a good judge of men, had no trouble coming up with his assessment this time — calm, straightforward, and deadly.

Barley brought the pails and the

federal deputy helped Hatfield carry them across to the jailhouse, but the federal officer lingered in the office, over by the rack of guns, until Hatfield returned from poking the little pails under each cell door. Orcutt and Horne were hungry, and silent. Henry Schmidt's mouth was too sore, and he did not appear to have much of an appetite anyway.

When Hatfield returned and closed the cell-room door, he gestured for Charley Wheaton to have a chair, and went over to sit at the desk, and wait.

The federal peace officer offered Evan a cigar, which was declined, then lit one for himself, and with a bemused expression gazed over at Sheriff Hatfield. "A week back the Land Office in Denver got a letter from some settlers, Sheriff. It said the law down here in Lost Valley wouldn't let the homesteaders go onto their land. The federal marshal sent me down to look around."

Evan eased the chair around a little so he was fully facing the federal officer, then he leaned back slightly to get comfortable, and started reciting everything that had happened up to the battle in the roadway this morning. The only thing he left out was his last discussion with Douglas Hyland. When he had finished, the cigar-smoking, calm man over by the door said: "Well, Sheriff, those people have title to the land."

"So does Mister Hyland, Marshal. I just told you . . . all I'm trying to do is keep the peace until Mister Hyland gets back. Then we'll know whose title is good."

"I saw the maps of government land up in Denver, Sheriff."

"Fine. Did you look up the titles for the land down here?"

Wheaton removed the cigar before replying. "No. But the clerks up there told me. . . ."

"Marshal, clerks make mistakes. We all do. But even if they didn't make any, until Mister Hyland gets home with the results of his title search, no one trespasses on Hyland range, because, if they do, Mister Hyland's range riders are going to chouse them off, and that's exactly what I'm trying to prevent . . . someone getting killed."

Charley Wheaton examined the gray ash of his cigar for a moment before speaking again. "When will Mister Hyland get back, Sheriff?"

"By my calculations, maybe tomorrow. I sure hope to hell it's tomorrow. I'm getting worn to a frazzle keeping people apart. And you might as well know, because the settlers'll tell you anyway, last night I led a posse to steal their horses, fetch them back to town, and impound them."

Wheaton's gray eyes lifted from the end of his cigar. "You served impounding papers on them?"

Hatfield curbed his rising temper. "No, sir, and, if I had, they'd have shot me off my horse. One son-of-a-bitch was ready to shoot me yesterday just for trying to talk sense to them."

Marshal Wheaton went back to examining the cigar ash as he quietly said: "You better make out those papers and serve them, Sheriff, otherwise those people can swear out a warrant against you for horse stealing."

Evan smiled without a shred of humor. "There's no one to serve it, Marshal. I'm the only lawman in Lost Valley."

Wheaton's gray eyes swept up again. "You *were* the only lawman in Lost Valley, Sheriff."

Hatfield's antagonism was increasing by the moment. Marshal Wheaton's hint of condescension, his imperturbability, and now his hint about using his federal powers in something he knew almost nothing about, while Evan Hatfield had been bearing all the danger — and pain — made the sheriff sit there, staring at the other man. Finally he said: "Marshal, did you ever hear the story about that old Texas Ranger who rode over a hill with his men and came onto a big band of Mex raiders?"

Wheaton shook his head.

"Well, Marshal, the old Texan looked at the Mexicans, who were looking at him and his men, then the old ranger looked up and said . . . 'Lord, please be on our side, but, Lord, if you can't do that, then please, sir, go over and set under that tree out of the way, and watch the damnedest fight you ever saw.' "

Wheaton smiled, removed his stogie, and unwound gracefully up out of the chair. "I gather from that, Sheriff, that you're telling me to go sit under a tree, and stay out of this until it's settled."

Evan stood up, too, and smiled back. "Something like that, Marshal."

They went out front where afternoon shadows were thickening. The federal officer looked up and down the roadway, plugged the stogie back into his mouth, and said: "You have a nice town here, Sheriff." He strode northward in the direction of the rooming house.

Hatfield returned to his chair, gingerly probed some sore ribs, then searched among his drawers for one of the blank printed forms to be filled out for the impounding of livestock. He took fifteen minutes to fill the thing in and make a copy of it, then he went down into the cell room, and, when Henry Schmidt responded to Hatfield's order to approach the door of the cell, Hatfield shoved the paper through. Schmidt took it, frowned downward, then looked out at Hatfield. "What's this?"

"Legal notice that I'm going to impound your livestock."

"You already have them."

Hatfield leaned on the door. "Yeah. But this makes it legal." He and Schmidt exchanged a long look, while behind them across the little aisle Orcutt and William Horne were hanging on each word. Hatfield said: "You feeling all right?"

Schmidt's one good eye hardened. "Better'n you're feeling!"

Hatfield smiled a little. "You might be right at that. You hit hard."

"So do you."

"You're more experienced at that kind of fighting than I am."

"I've done my share of it, Sheriff."

"For money, Mister Schmidt?"

"Yes."

Hatfield and the bull-necked man continued to regard each other for a moment, then the sheriff said: "You want another drink of branch water and medicine?"

For the first time since they had met, Henry Schmidt's gaze showed something else besides violent dislike and antagonism. Even his voice was different. "I'd admire that, Sheriff."

Hatfield fished out the brass key, wordlessly unlocked the cell door, and led the way back up to the office. Orcutt and Horne watched in silence, then exchanged a long look of disbelief.

Henry Schmidt went to the same wall bench where he had sat before, and waited until the sheriff had doctored two glasses of malt whiskey with creek water, then Schmidt tasted his, licked his lips with care because one side of his mouth was swollen, and fixed Hatfield with his one good eye. "You could fight for money," he said. "You gave me the best fight I ever had from someone who's never climbed into a ring."

Hatfield chuckled. "No, thanks. About one more like that, Mister Schmidt, and I'd be riding a wheelchair." He sipped his drink. "Not bad whiskey, is it? I get a bottle every now and then when a freighter named Gallatin comes through the valley."

Schmidt ignored the comment about the whiskey. He drank it slowly, and leaned against the wall, gazing over at Hatfield. "You trying to soften me up, Sheriff?"

"Nope. I just figured you might ache as much as I do."

"But you're still Hyland's man."

"I never was Mister Hyland's man. I've known him a few years. He's tough, but he's fair and honest as the day is long. I've said it a dozen times, but I'll say it again . . . all I'm doing is keeping the peace. That's all I aim to do until Mister Hyland gets back. After that, if his title's no good, I'll personally ride with you folks to your homesteads. If it is good, I'll give you back your horses along with one day to get off his range. Care for a refill?"

Schmidt looked into his empty glass for a moment before answering. "No thanks. One more and I'd have to crawl back to the cell down on all fours." He looked up. "I think you're going to win, Sheriff."

Hatfield swished the dregs in his glass. "Mister Schmidt, pass me your word you won't make any more trouble, and I'll loan you a horse to get back to your family." Hatfield put aside the glass.

The battered settler was slow to answer. "You got my word, Sheriff."

Hatfield arose, fished in his desk for Schmidt's personal possessions, then waited, and, when the settler had everything shoved back into his pockets, Hatfield led the way down to the livery barn. Over in front of the general store several loafers slouching in the shade, stared, and one man said: "I'll be damned, will you look there? They was trying to beat each other to death this morning."

XIV

Without Hatfield's knowledge the federal deputy marshal hired a horse and rode down along Arapaho Creek. He spent a couple of hours there and was making a leisurely return to town when he was halted by converging range men. Joe Lamont led them, and evidently Joe had watched the marshal go down to the creek, and had waited to waylay him on the ride back.

By the time Charley Wheaton reached Hyland, it was suppertime, and, although Marshal Wheaton ate at Barley Smith's counter, he missed encountering the sheriff by a half hour. They did not meet until after nightfall when Marshal Wheaton visited the saloon for a nightcap and met Sheriff Hatfield at the bar. Wheaton took a bottle, invited Hatfield to a table, and, when they were comfortable, Wheaton related his adventure.

Hatfield sat in silence until Wheaton was finished, then looked stonily at the federal officer. "I thought you were going to stay in town, Marshal."

Wheaton was refilling his little shot glass when he answered. "That was your idea, not mine." He leaned also to refill Hatfield's glass. "My job is to find out what's happening down here. I got your version this morning and their version this afternoon." He raised his glance, smiling. "And while I didn't figure on it, I got the cattlemen's version, too." Wheaton raised his head, dropped the whiskey straight down, and did not even blink as he set his empty glass aside, and felt inside his coat for a stogie. "If you're waiting for my judgment, Sheriff, I don't have one. Nobody around here seems to be exactly wearing a halo." He lit up. "And if Hyland returns tomorrow, that should pretty well settle the main issue."

Hatfield raised his glass, downed its contents, and blew out a flammable breath. "If . . . ," he said. Wheaton gazed over at him so he finished it. "If Mister Hyland returns tomorrow."

"You got doubts, Sheriff?"

"No, not about his intentions, but things don't always work out the way we want them to, do they, Marshal?"

Wheaton trickled smoke. "I sure hope he returns tomorrow, Sheriff, because an awful lot of people are expecting him to, and, if he don't, it's going to aggravate conditions, isn't it?"

Evan did not answer the question. He had just glanced up in time to see those two settlers named Dent and Arbuckle walk in. There was something about those two. There had been something when they'd first walked into his office, but he could not pin it down except that they only half resembled settlers; otherwise, they left Hatfield with a feeling that they were stockmen, or at least had been stockmen. Nor was it simply because they wore shell belts and six-guns. It was the way they wore them.

Marshal Wheaton caught Hatfield's attention with a question. "Those two are men you know, Sheriff?"

"Met them this afternoon. They're settlers. At least that's what they told me, but the settlers I've met lately don't commonly carry guns or look quite as natural atop saddle horses."

Wheaton watched Arbuckle and Dent approach the bar, removed his cigar, and said: "Up north, where there's a lot more homesteading, we see quite a few like that pair. Range riders turned settlers. A hundred and sixty acres of decent land beats riding in blistering heat and blizzards for ten dollars a month, Sheriff."

Hatfield shoved out his legs under the table and continued to watch Arbuckle and Dent, but only peripherally because Marshal Wheaton was speaking again.

"You remind me of the little Dutch kid who shoved his thumb in the dike, Sheriff. You're stopping settlers from going up Arapaho Creek, and meanwhile more settlers are arriving . . . like those two at the bar. It's called progress."

Hatfield shook his head. "Growth, Marshal, not progress."

Wheaton accepted that in his unruffled manner. "Growth. All right, we'll call it growth, and, Sheriff, I can tell you that for every one you hold back, ten more are on the way. By next autumn you'll have 'em camping around your town like honey bees at a rose bush. You can't dam them up east of the stage road."

"I don't mean to. I wouldn't have done it this time, if there hadn't been damned good reason to do it. By next summer we'll know where they can squat and where they can't."

Wheaton's steady gaze was unwavering. "That's not exactly what I meant, Sheriff. I mean that right now you're protecting Hyland's range. Next summer it will be other cowmen. Maybe Hyland, too, but the other stockmen in Lost Valley. You'll be standing there with your thumb shoved in the dike trying to hold back the sea."

Hatfield sighed. "You didn't understand a damned thing I told you today, Marshal. I'm not protecting Hyland as much as I'm trying to protect those damned settlers. As for the other cowmen . . . if settlers roll in with clear titles to land, legal titles, my job will be to see that their legal rights are protected."

"Can you do it, Sheriff?"

"Why don't we wait until it happens

and see if I can do it, Marshal?"

Wheaton removed his stogie to comment when several loud, rough voices over at the bar overrode all the quieter voices in the room and Hatfield swung to look. He knew the angry cowboy, not by name but by sight, who was easing away from the bar as he faced Arbuckle and Dent. The man worked for an outfit called Cedarbrake, which lay about twelve miles southeast of town and was owned by a corporation of Eastern investors. There were two other Cedarbrake range men along the bar, but they were northward, behind Dent and Arbuckle, and, although they had turned at the sounds of friction, so far they had not moved. Still, what bothered Evan Hatfield was that this was how killings occurred — one man in front holding attention, and two men behind in the crowd.

Hatfield shoved up to his feet as the angry cowboy said: "You goddamned squatters got no right in here anyhow. You're supposed to be drinkin' swill at the trough with the other pigs."

Hatfield was moving before Cal Arbuckle, who was closest to the red-faced Cedarbrake rider, stepped sideways away from the bar in order to have moving room. Into the sudden barroom hush Arbuckle said: "You're forcing this, mister."

The cowboy sneered. "You clod-hopping bastard!"

One of the other Cedarbrake riders farther along the bar raised a hand in warning, trying to convey by gesture that someone was coming up behind the settler-baiting range man.

Arbuckle took down a shallow breath. Hatfield could see that while he was still ten feet from the Cedarbrake rider. Arbuckle was going to fight. In a clear, rough voice of command Hatfield closed the distance in three big strides and rammed a six-gun muzzle into the back of the Cedarbrake range man. "You get on your horse, mister, get out of Hyland, and don't you ever come back."

No one moved. The other patrons were as hushed and motionless as stone. Harry Dent, behind Arbuckle along the bar, had a hand on his gun butt. Those other two Cedarbrake men were standing the same way, undecided and intently watchful. One of them moved a little and from over by the door a voice came as distinct and cold as steel balls falling on glass spoke.

"Take your hand off that gun . . . you, with the red shirt!"

Eyes swiveled in that direction, but otherwise none of the patrons moved. The cowboy in the red shirt lifted his gun hand very slowly and draped it over the bar top. The man by the door shifted his stogie from one side of his mouth to the other side. He was holding a long-barreled Colt.

Hatfield reached around to lift away the gun of the man he was covering, and the cowboy whirled with a hay-making wild swing. Hatfield was already leaning so he simply leaned lower to allow the arm to sail above, then he caught cloth in his reaching hand, yanked the red-faced man around, and swung his six-gun sideways to the temple. The Cedarbrake cowboy went down in a heap in the sawdust of the bar room floor.

These other two Cedarbrake men wilted. They hadn't really been prepared anyway when their half-drunk friend picked the fight.

Every eye in the crowded saloon went from the unconscious man at Hatfield's feet to the cigar-smoking stranger over by the door with the long-barreled six-gun.

The barman made a perfunctory sweep of the worn wood in front of him with his bar rag, then leaned to look down at the unconscious man. "He always drinks too much," the barman plaintively said into the silence.

Hatfield ignored that and growled at the pair of Cedarbrake men behind

Dent. "Pick up your friend and haul him back to the ranch. And keep him there. Tell the range boss I don't want to see him back here in town. Get him out of here!"

Gradually, as the unconscious man was hoisted and balanced between his friends to be taken out into the star-bright night, the saloon returned almost to normal, but it would not actually be normal again tonight. Hatfield's annoyance, the efficient way he had downed the fighting cowboy, was only part of what super-seded all other matters under discussion along the bar and among the tables. The other subject was the identity of that cigar-smoking stranger with the fast draw and the long-barreled Colt.

But Wheaton seemed ignorant of

being the focal point for a lot of sidelong looks as he resumed his chair at the table and poured both their glasses full again. Then he smiled over at Hatfield and said: "Here's hoping you'll always be able to get a handle on them, Sheriff. You did that right well."

Hatfield did not smile back as he ignored the glass and said: "Thanks for the help." Then he leaned to arise and head for the rooming house. "And I'm right obliged for the whiskey."

Charley Wheaton nodded, pulled on his cigar, and watched the sheriff's departure through narrowed eyes, impervious to the glances he was getting.

Hatfield paused to breathe deeply of fresh night air when Cal Arbuckle walked out behind him and said: "I guess that was the best way to end it, Sheriff, but the damned fool deserved shooting."

Hatfield turned. He was tired, his body ached, and right now he was sick and tired of looking at settlers, so he said: "Mister, no half-drunk feller deserves shooting, not even a silly one like that bastard. Good night."

Hatfield crossed the road and went up to the rooming house. The uppermost saving thought in his mind as he got ready for bed was that tomorrow Douglas Hyland would return. Then, one way or the other, this whole damned oversize headache would be resolved. And if he didn't return?

Hatfield dropped his head upon the

pillow completely unwilling to believe that. When Douglas Hyland said he would be back in two weeks, a man could count on it to the day. With that thought firmly in mind, Hatfield fell asleep — and snored.

When he awakened, hours later, and moved, his muscles ached almost as much as they had right after the fight, but by the time he had shaved, dressed, and was ready for breakfast down at Barley's place, he had warmed out of the stiffness like an old horse.

Orcutt and Horne greeted him with loud demands to be released as he had released Henry Schmidt, and he ignored them until the pails had been shoved under each door, then he stood up, looking benign, said nothing, and retreated back to the office.

Not until the liveryman came shoving in breathlessly to report that someone had stolen those impounded settler horses did Hatfield's firm conviction that this was to be a good day for him begin to waver.

He returned southward with the agitated liveryman, walked all around the empty corrals, decided that reading sign in an area where everyone wore those flat-heeled freighter-type cowhide boots was a waste of time, and growled for his horse to be saddled, then strode back to the jailhouse for his Winchester.

He was emerging with the booted saddle gun draped in one bent arm and encountered the federal marshal. Wheaton raised one eyebrow. "Indians coming, Sheriff?"

Hatfield was not in a facetious

mood. "Those blasted settlers stole back their horses last night."

As he turned to stride southward, Marshal Wheaton fell in beside him. "Could it have been someone else, Sheriff? It didn't have to be the squatters, did it?"

Hatfield turned a vinegary expression upon the marshal. "No, it didn't have to be. It could have been the Four Horsemen of the Apocalypse. They got bucked off while riding through the sky last night and stole the settlers' horses for replacements."

Wheaton said no more. When Evan Hatfield buckled the boot into place on the underside of his rosadero, then led the horse out back before mounting, Marshal Wheaton stood like a preacher with both hands clasped together under his coat in back, watching. As soon as Hatfield rode away, the marshal collared the liveryman and ordered a livery animal brought up and saddled for him.

Hatfield looped his reins, rolled and lit a smoke, and sniffed the morning air. It had a slightly metallic scent to it. He scanned the sky, found some soiled remnants of clouds a long way off northward, and decided it was going to rain, if not tonight, then tomorrow.

The land was empty as usual; the grass was beginning to head out and cure on the stalk. Autumn was not far off, a couple of months away. Hatfield decided to follow the land swells and, while doing this, caught sight of distant movement, men and horses heading in his direction. He walked his horse along, watching in puzzled interest because, although he could make out the horses fairly well, they did not all seem to be under saddle. Perhaps four or five of them were riderless among a pair of riders. His first thought was that Lamont had led a raid and had come off second best. Then, as he stood in his stirrups, something compelled him to look back. Marshal Wheaton was cantering easily along in Hatfield's wake.

He halted, sat flat down, and waited. By the time the federal deputy came up, those other horsemen were a mile closer, and Wheaton pointed in their direction. "Bringing them back, Sheriff."

He was correct. Hatfield said nothing as the two of them turned to intercept the distant horses. Henry

Schmidt, unmistakable in build even in the saddle, was herding the same livestock ahead of him that Sheriff Hatfield and his posse men had gone to such trouble to steal a couple of nights back. Riding in the drag, looking dejected, was one of those sorrel-headed gangling youths, the son of incarcerated William Horne.

Hatfield halted, looped his reins, and leaned upon the saddle horn, waiting. When Schmidt arrived, he looked with interest at Marshal Wheaton, then ignored him to nod to Hatfield as he said: "Our horses must have got out last night and headed for home."

Hatfield was staring at the crestfallen youth. No horse got out of those public corrals without some two-legged help.

"We caught them a couple of hours back," stated Henry Schmidt, "and was bringing them back."

Hatfield continued to lean and gaze at the self-conscious tall youth. Then he shifted his attention to Schmidt, whose closed eye was purple and slightly less swollen today, but was still tightly closed. For a moment they regarded one another before the sheriff gruffly spoke.

"Take 'em back with you, Mister Schmidt. It's too long a drive back to town, so keep them down there with you folks."

They continued to look at one another. Schmidt finally said: "We're right obliged, Mister Hatfield."

Evan ignored that to say: "Don't drape any harness on them."

Schmidt nodded. "We'll be right

where we are now when you come back, Mister Hatfield." Then he considered the federal officer and said: "The womenfolk are getting breakfast, if you gents are hungry."

Hatfield lifted his reins. "Thanks all the same but we've eaten." Then he looked stonily at the gangling youth. "Boy, the next time you get a bright idea like that, you ask some older man first. You understand me?"

The sorrel-headed youth got red in the face. "Yes, sir, I understand you."

Hatfield bobbed his head at Henry Schmidt and turned to ride back toward town. Charley Wheaton, who had not opened his mouth back there, did not open it now until they had roof tops in sight. Then he yawned, stretched, looked at the sky, the rolling miles of rangeland, and said: "Sheriff, like I already said, I think you'll make it work."

XV

Something happened before noon that ordinarily did not bother folks in Hyland. It rarely bothered the sheriff, either. The morning stage from the north was late.

Hatfield stopped by the corral yard and spoke briefly with the company's local supervisor on his way back to the livery barn. All the stage man could say was that he'd been told by the previous driver from up north that there had been some bad flash floods over in the direction of Denver. Hatfield and Wheaton walked their horses down to the barn, handed them to the day men, and started back toward the jailhouse. Wheaton said: "It's still early, Sheriff."

Hatfield fired up his stove, put new grounds in the pot, filled it with water, and set it atop the solitary burner of his wood stove, then he tossed down his hat and gazed at Marshal Wheaton. "And suppose Mister Hyland's titles are good?"

The marshal's concern had never been anything but clinical. "Then the squatters along the creek will have to leave."

Hatfield went to his desk, sat down, heard noise in the roadway, and sprang up to step to a front window, and peer out. The morning stage had just made its big swing up the road to enter the palisaded corral yard. He stood a moment in thought, then went to the stove to poke in another piece of wood, which was not needed, lifted the lid of the coffee pot, peered in, replaced the lid, and went back to his desk. Marshal Wheaton watched all this wearing an expression of faint amusement.

Minutes passed before Hatfield heard boot steps approaching out front. They stopped, a strong hand lifted his latch, and shoved the door in. Hatfield started to arise, then froze where he was standing. The newcomer was a total stranger. He was pale-eyed with a droopy cavalry-man's moustache, and had an ivory-stocked six-gun tied to his right leg. He held the door aside, nodded at Wheaton and Hatfield, then moved slightly to one side as Douglas Hyland walked in.

Hyland looked drawn. His clothes were rumpled. His normally craggy, rough-set features were flaccid as he stepped into the room and nodded at Evan Hatfield, then eyed Marshal Wheaton. Before he could speak, the stranger with the cavalryman's moustache said: "Charley . . . they said you'd be down here."

Wheaton arose. "Sheriff Hatfield, this is Sam Hinkley, deputy U.S. marshal out of Denver. Sam, Sheriff Evan Hatfield."

The pale-eyed man stepped ahead and pumped Hatfield's hand, then stepped back as Douglas Hyland pulled a chair around and sank into it. "Evan, everything all right?"

Hatfield felt for the chair behind him. "No, everything isn't all right."

Hyland accepted that as though he

had expected no other answer. "Do you have a shot around the office, Evan?"

Hatfield leaned far down, drew forth his malt whiskey, and set up a couple of shot glasses. Hyland came over, poured himself a jolt, swallowed it, refilled the glass, and returned to the chair, holding it.

Hatfield was beginning to feel as though someone had yanked out the ground from under him. Hyland motioned for Marshal Sam Hinkley to help himself to a shot, too, but Hinkley remained over by the door, evidently willing to be an onlooker now, as Douglas Hyland reached inside his rumpled coat and brought forth some carefully folded papers that he held on his lap as he said: "Mister Hinkley and I've been riding stages since day before yesterday. When I was thirty years younger, getting bruised and shaken didn't bother me. I could sleep on a stagecoach. But not any more." He leaned to pitch the papers atop Hatfield's desk, downed his second jolt of whiskey, and seemed to revive.

Evan considered the folded papers, several of which were maps. He knew the answer was in them, but he preferred hearing it from the man they called the lord of Lost Valley. "Did you get it settled?" Hatfield asked quietly, clasping both hands atop the desk.

Hyland blew out a whiskey breath before answering. "Yes. It took three days but it's settled. My deeds are perfectly legal."

Hatfield loosened slightly. "Those

land people up in Denver were wrong, then?"

"Not exactly, Evan. In fact, the titles they issued were proper and all . . . they just were issued for the wrong township. Someone didn't complete a file search of old deeds. In Denver they said that happened in Omaha, but my guess is that in Omaha they'd say it happened in Denver, but the main point is my land legally belongs to Lost Valley Ranch."

Charley Wheaton glanced up at Marshal Hinkley. "They sent you along to verify this, Sam?"

Hinkley's answer was ambiguous. "They told me to come down here with Mister Hyland to verify it, yes, but they also said you were likely to need help. How many settlers have we got on Mister Hyland's range?"

Wheaton looked at Hatfield for the answer to that. Evan let go a long breath, then eased back in his chair. "They won't be troublesome, Mister Hinkley. There are three wagons of them along Arapaho Creek on Mister Hyland's range, and I've got a couple more locked in my cells."

Douglas Hyland stared at Hatfield. "Three wagons of them on my range, Evan?"

Charley Wheaton spoke first. "Mister Hyland, Sheriff Hatfield did a hell of a job keeping your riders and those settlers from going at it, and in the process he got threatened with guns, and damned near whipped in a fist fight. I'd say you owe him a big load of thanks."

Hyland listened to this, then

gripped the little shot glass in his fist, and scowled at it.

Hatfield, who knew Douglas Hyland as well as anyone did, guessed what thoughts were going through the older man's mind. Douglas Hyland might be tired, worn down, and right now feeling the subdued fire of two jolts of whiskey, but he was still flinty, unyielding Douglas Hyland, and trespassers on his range, regardless of the circumstances, were intolerable to him. When he raised his eyes, Hatfield was waiting to say: "You don't just climb on a stage and head for Albuquerque, then over to Denver, and expect everything here to remain the same when you damned well knew there were settlers coming. Maybe someday when I feel like it, I'll tell you the whole story.

Right now, Douglas, we'll ride down there and let the marshals tell those folks they're in the wrong township, and you can get a little taste of how they feel."

But Hyland was not ready to go anywhere except to his home place. As he arose, he pointed to the copies of maps and deeds atop the desk. "Keep them, Evan. Right now I'm going home to sleep for a couple of days." He turned toward the door, then glanced back. "Step out front with me for a moment, will you?"

Hatfield arose and walked around the desk to comply. Outside, those distant soiled clouds were beginning to fill up and broaden, otherwise the afternoon was a little warmer than the morning had been and everything else seemed about the same.

Inside, Marshal Hinkley finally stepped to the desk to fill a glass from Hatfield's bottle, then he faced Charley Wheaton. "That's a tough old man, that Hyland."

Wheaton had a judgment of his own to offer. "Hatfield's more than tough, Sam. He's tough and sensible."

Hinkley downed the whiskey and made a face. Then he said: "How many of these clod-hoppers are we going to have trouble with?"

"Serious trouble, none, Sam. Hatfield broke 'em to lead one at a time. I'll tell you about it on the ride back to Denver."

Hinkley considered refilling his glass, gave up the idea, and said: "You're to go back, Charley. I'm to go on down to Raton where a pair of

Chihuahua renegades named Jensen and Rowe have been stealing horses and cattle and driving them down over the line."

Outside in the pleasant sunlight with the busy town handily ignoring them as they leaned upon the tie rack, Douglas Hyland was frowning at the ground as he spoke.

"It was a damned close thing, Evan. My grandfather recorded the old Mexican deeds in Albuquerque . . . in Spanish. Just by damned good luck did those old files get turned over to the Americans when we took over this country out here, but no one could read them and some got thrown out and burned. Mine happened to be saved. It was nothing but luck." Hyland raised his face. "I worried about you and Joe up here. That feller inside was right, I'm sure of it . . . you kept the peace. About those squatters along the creek . . . I'll ride down there with you tomorrow."

Hatfield said: "No, you won't, Douglas. So far I've been getting by on the skin of my teeth, because I could guess about how people would act. It's been touch and go, but so far no one's got shot."

"What's that got to do with me going down there with you tomorrow?"

"A lot. I know you as well as I know myself. Those folks aren't going to like what the marshals tell them. If you were along and they got rough in their talk, you'd send your riding crew to visit them. That's been your reaction to trespassers ever since I've been in this country. But not tomorrow, Douglas, not any more at all. I'll go down there with the marshals in the morning. We'll get it all settled and get those folks to move back east of the road."

Douglas Hyland said nothing for a long moment while he gazed at Evan Hatfield, then slowly his craggy face split into a rare, flinty smile, and he pushed out a hand. "I never doubted for long that you'd be able to handle it, Evan. Not for very long. Come by the ranch in a day or two and we'll have supper and some whiskey afterward, and talk. Agreed?"

Hatfield nodded, watched Douglas Hyland head south to hire a horse at the livery barn, and remained standing in the warming sunlight for several minutes afterward, before he reëntered the jailhouse office to make plans for the morning ride down along Arapaho Creek with the two federal deputy marshals.

Maybe he should have been a harness maker, after all. It was going to be raining cats and dogs in the morning, and he knew it. Harness makers did not have to ride through rainstorms to carry unwelcome news to folks.

ABOUT THE AUTHOR

Lauran Paine who, under his own name and various pseudonyms has written over a thousand books, was born in Duluth, Minnesota. His family moved to California when he was at a young age and his apprenticeship as a Western writer came about through the years he spent in the livestock trade, rodeos, and even motion pictures where he served as an extra because of his expert horsemanship in several films starring movie cowboy Johnny Mack Brown. In the late 1930s, Paine trapped wild horses in northern Arizona and even, for a time, worked as a professional far-rier. Paine came to know the Old West through the eyes of many who had been born in the previous century, and he learned that Western life had been very different from the way it was portrayed on the screen. "I knew men who had killed other men," he later recalled. "But they were the exceptions. Prior to and during the Depression, people were just too busy eking out an existence to indulge in Saturday-night brawls." He served in the U.S. Navy in the Second World War and began writing for Western pulp magazines following his discharge. It is interesting to note that all of his earliest novels (written under his own name and the pseudo-nym Mark Carrel) were published in the British market and he soon had as strong a following in that country as in the United States. Paine's Western fiction is characterized by strong plots, authenticity, an apparently effortless ability to construct situation and character, and a preference for building his stories upon a solid foundation of historical fact. *Adobe Empire* (1956), one of his best novels, is a fictionalized account of the last twenty years in the life of trader William Bent and, in an off-trail way, has a melancholy, bittersweet texture that is not easily forgotten. In later novels like *Cache Cañon* (Five Star Westerns, 1998) and *Halfmoon Ranch* (Five Star Westerns, 2007), he showed that the special magic and power of his stories and characters had only matured along with his basic themes of changing times, changing attitudes, learning from experience, respecting Nature, and the yearning for a simpler, more moderate way of life.

The employees of Thorndike Press hope you have enjoyed this Large Print book. All our Thorndike, Wheeler, and Kennebec Large Print titles are designed for easy reading, and all our books are made to last. Other Thorndike Press Large Print books are available at your library, through selected bookstores, or directly from us.

For information about titles, please call:
  (800) 223-1244

or visit our Web site at:
  http://gale.cengage.com/thorndike

To share your comments, please write:
  Publisher
  Thorndike Press
  10 Water St., Suite 310
  Waterville, ME 04901